THE LAST MUSKETEER

JANE CORBETT

Beggar Books

First published in 2020 by Beggar Books
Copyright © Jane Corbett 2020
The right of Jane Corbett to be identified as the author of this work has
been asserted by her in accordance with the Copyright, Designs and
Patents Act 1988.
A CIP catalogue record for this book is available from the British
Library.
ISBN: 978-1-910852-84-2
eISBN: 978-1-910852-83-5
Cover image and design by Jamie Keenan
Typeset by Yen Ooi

THE LAST MUSKETEER

A young woman clad in biking leathers descended the steps of a tall terraced house on the sea front at Dún Laoghaire. She extracted a helmet from the compartment beneath the seat of her motorbike parked next to a hedge of wild fuchsia, strapped it on and mounted the bike. Shards of light broke through an overcast sky, glinting here and there off a sluggish grey sea. After another mile, she turned onto the motorway. Most of the traffic was moving in the opposite direction, so she opened up the throttle and the bike leapt forward with a surge of speed.

In barely ten minutes the business park was signposted, and a cluster of gleaming new buildings rose up ahead. She took the turn-off, and a few moments later she entered the car park of one of the international companies lured to Ireland by generous tax incentives. The building was painted white in the style of 1920s Art Deco to resemble an ocean-going liner, with metal windows and a flat roof. She looked at her watch. The journey had taken less than fifteen minutes, and she was twenty minutes early for her first day as assistant to the manager of R and D at Associated Swiss Pharmaceuticals. It was a step up from her previous job as trainee accountant, but still not the economist she hoped to become. It was also a homecoming to her father's land.

———

The sound of a motorbike, a Yamaha R3 if he wasn't mistaken, drew Conrad Dreyer to his office window. He'd had a passion for bikes ever since boyhood, and as soon as he could he bought one cheap to travel the dusty roads of some North African desert region, until eventually the engine burned out. It was high time, he thought, for another.

He watched the rider pull up in a parking space and dismount, a small person for such a solid bike. As they removed the helmet and shook out a mop of curly black hair, he noticed with mild surprise that the rider was a woman. She paused to look into one of the bike's side mirrors, took out a lipstick from her pocket and applied it carefully. Then with practised efficiency she divested herself of boots and leathers, and shoved them with her helmet into the luggage compartment at the back of the bike. Intrigued, he continued to observe her as she walked towards the front of the building, texting as she went, and was lost to sight.

———

S imon entered the kitchen of the brand new sixth floor apartment he shared with his friend Jonas.

'Not raining for once!' Jonas said cheerfully. 'A quick coffee before we go?'

Simon glanced at the expensive coffee machine that stood waiting on the gleaming counter.

'Not with that thing. It'll take too long. I just heard from Fela. She's arrived. We need to go if we're to catch her before she gets stuck in with Dreyer.'

Jonas sighed. 'I don't understand your disdain for mod cons.'

'If you mean this soulless machine for living, you're right.'

'After the shitholes we've put up with, I for one appreciate a bit of luxury. Not to mention the view.'

Simon glanced out through the window at the dim outline of the Wicklow hills.

'That, I grant you, is worth it. Let's go.'

They'd met as postgraduate students in the Department of Biotechnology at Newcastle University, where for the last two years of their Ph.D. studies they shared a flat, though Jonas referred to it as a squat. Simon specialised in diseases prevalent in developing countries, with a view to creating effective vaccines – something equally relevant to their current living conditions, according to his flatmates. Jonas's research was concerned principally with plants, their resistance to disease and how their yield might be increased in poor growing conditions. On achieving their doctorates, Associated Swiss Pharmaceuticals had offered them both jobs in their expanding R and D department – the opportunity to continue their research for a generous salary, plus a flat for modest rent in a newly completed block a stone's throw from the company premises. They felt like kings.

———

The security guard nodded a greeting as Fela entered the foyer. The tasteful flower arrangements, cream leather sofas and low glass-topped tables with offerings of up-to-date lifestyle and scientific magazines completed the impression of opulence. She gave her name to the girl on reception, who greeted her with a friendly smile.

'Felicity O'Connor? Welcome to Associated Swiss Pharmaceuticals!'

She produced a visitor's pass card attached to a ribbon from beneath the counter and handed it to Fela. 'I'll have your own card for you by the end of the day. Your office is on the third floor. "Finance and Planning." It's clearly marked. There's a lift over there.'

Fela got out at the third floor and walked down a wide corridor till she came to the right door. She knocked and waited. She'd forgotten the name of the Swiss man who'd interviewed her on Skype, and was suddenly overtaken by nerves.

A voice called out. 'Come in!'

The figure standing at the desk was silhouetted against the window overlooking the car park, and at first she was unable to make out his features. As she walked towards him, the name Weiss surfaced. She held out her hand and said quickly, 'Dr Weiss! It's good to meet you in the flesh at last!'

The man emerged from behind the desk and his face came into focus.

'Conrad Dreyer,' he said, taking her outstretched hand. 'Dr Weiss is our CEO. I'm here to balance the books. You'll be working with me.'

She smiled in an attempt to cover her embarrassment.

'Can I get you a coffee?'

'Thanks. Milk, no sugar.'

She observed him as he went over to the table on the far side of the room, where a coffee machine and cups stood waiting. He was of medium height, with thick reddish-brown hair and eyes the colour of anthracite. She guessed he was in his mid-forties, though his weather-beaten features made him look older. He came towards her, holding out a mug.

'I hope you received the dossier I sent you?'

'I downloaded something from an email, if that's what you mean?'

'Our secretarial section seems to be undergoing some sort of crisis. I've got a printed copy here.'

He went over to a filing cabinet, brought out a file and handed it to her. 'Scan it at your leisure. Your office is through here.'

He moved with a swiftness that made the space suddenly contract and opened the door to the adjacent room. 'It's small, but at least you can open the window. Not always the case with these modern buildings. Make yourself at home. When you're ready, come back here and we can talk.'

He pulled the door to close behind him and she found herself alone. Dr Dreyer didn't appear to go in for small talk, unlike her previous boss in the accountancy firm with his constant complaints about commuter trains and the problems of his domestic life.

————

She did her best to take in the bewildering range of figures her job involved, and after a couple of hours Dreyer suggested they take a break. As they entered the canteen on the ground floor, she saw Simon and Jonas seated at a corner table. They waved to her as she sat down, and Dreyer went over to the counter. He returned with coffees and a couple of pastries and took a seat opposite her.

'Have you found somewhere to live yet? I apologise for not offering you a company flat, but it seems they're limited to researchers. They often work extra-long hours.'

'I've found a place in Dún Laoghaire. I know it from when I was a child and I like it there.'

He nodded. 'Good! And I see you've got transport.'

'My bike. Yes, it makes the journey easy.'

Their talk quickly ran out, and she was relieved when he finished his coffee and got up. 'I need to get back to my desk, but you take your time.'

As soon as he'd gone, she went over to join Simon and Jonas.

'At last! Sorry we missed you this morning,' Simon said, getting up and giving her a bear hug.

Jonas embraced her too and they sat down.

'What d'you think of the place?' Jonas asked eagerly.

'Very glitzy!'

'Well run, too. So you're not sorry we persuaded you to apply for the job?'

'It'll be a challenge.'

'That's what you wanted,' said Simon.

'I certainly couldn't have endured another year in the last place.'

'Things are moving here in Ireland. Though it's a shame they didn't offer you a flat,' said Jonas.

'In your high-rise monstrosity? I love my little eyrie.'

'They could put me in a hut in the garden and I'd be just as happy. Happier!' said Simon. 'Did you know Conrad's a fellow bike enthusiast?'

'Really? He didn't say.'

'He's not much of a conversationalist.'

'Preferable to Weiss,' said Jonas. 'Talks and talks and never listens to a word.'

The shutters on the canteen counter went up. Simon looked at his watch. 'Fancy some lunch? It's a bit early but I'm starving. And the food here's terrific.'

———

At the end of the day Fela decided to go straight home. Jonas had offered to cook dinner, but she asked for a rain check. She hadn't finished unpacking and could do with an early night. She suggested they might take a trip into town the following evening.

The sky was growing dark as she rode back to Dún Laoghaire, the horizon streaked with orange and duck egg blue as the sun sank behind the hills. She parked her bike outside her house and walked up the steps. At the top she paused to look out over the harbour. A ferry, all lit up, was making its laborious way to its berth, small boats bobbing wildly in its wake. The bustle of the quayside was infectious, and she felt hopeful in a way she hadn't since she and Simon broke up, more or less amicably, a little over a year ago.

The separation had hit her hard, even though they'd both known it wasn't working. It took her back to her parents' split, when she was nine years old and her world had cracked apart. Her father was a musician who travelled wherever his music took him. One day he stopped coming back at all, and the house in Battersea closed in on itself. While her mother busied herself with friends and her work as a newly qualified family lawyer, Fela stayed in alone, reading or doing homework at the kitchen table, jumping up to switch on the radio when eventually the silence rang out too loud.

Her mother was raised in Johannesburg, the first member of her family to go to university. They lived on the outskirts of the city, and every couple of years she and Fela went to visit her grandmother in a house full of the scents of exotic flowers and spicy cooking. Then, shortly after Fela's twelfth birthday, her grandmother died and the visits ceased.

Her father was from the west of Ireland and defied the conventions of his upbringing by marrying a black woman from Africa. She'd loved her Irish grandmother and their yearly visits to her village, though her mother never felt at ease there. As she grew into a teenager, however, the visits grew rarer. Being brought up in London she felt no deep connection to either the Irish or African sides of her family. Coming here offered a chance to rediscover her Irish roots.

In the hallway she was greeted by her elderly landlady, who was carrying a tray of tea from the kitchen into the sitting room. She and her husband had lived in the house all their married lives, and managed to hang onto it by turning the top floor into a separate flat. They liked the sounds of someone coming and going, they said. It gave the house life, and reminded them of the days when it was full of children. She made Fela think of her father's sister, the kindly aunt whose face she couldn't remember, in whose house she'd spent a couple of happy summers just up the coast.

The flat was small - bedroom, bathroom, tiny kitchen, and a living room with two mansard windows looking out to sea. She took off her biking leathers and left them in a pile near the front door. In the kitchen she uncorked a bottle of wine, poured herself a glass and decided to call her father. He was known as one of the finest fiddle players in Ireland and his band, The Bantry Boys, still filled every venue they played with fans old and new.

He was also a bike enthusiast, who from an early age had taught his daughter the joys of motorcycling. He kept his old Norton in a neighbour's garage next to the Dublin cottage he'd managed to hang onto on the north side of the Liffey in one of the rapidly gentrifying parts of the city. He complained the place no longer felt like home since many of the old residents moved out. There were still good people, though, prepared to look out for each other, who'd rallied round when he'd suffered a minor stroke and was forced to curtail his gypsy lifestyle.

'Hi, Da! It's me, Fela. What are you up to?'

'Fela, my darlin'! I thought you weren't coming till next week.'

At the sound of his voice tiredness left her.

'No, Da. I told you! Never mind. Are you at home? Can I drop by?'

'I'm sorry. I'm off to rehearse with the band in a few minutes. We've a gig coming up. I hope you'll be there.'

'Wouldn't miss it!'

'And bring your friends... Come over on Saturday. Not too early, mind. I'll give you your tea.'

'Okay. Teatime Saturday. And don't forget!'

'Would I ever? You're home now and we'll see a lot of us. How's your new job, by the way?'

'It's my first day. I'll tell you Saturday.'

'Grand! I'll be waiting.'

———

The following evening Simon was already seated when Fela arrived at a Vietnamese restaurant a few blocks from the company building.

'How did your second day go?' he asked, as she sat down.

'You can't believe the eye-watering budgets I'm working with.'

'With large chunks earmarked for my research, I hope. So don't balls it up.'

'Why d'you always make sarky remarks!'

'Irony, not sarcasm.'

'Same difference. They're put-downs.'

Simon waved to the waiter and ordered two glasses of wine.

'Don't get all prickly. What I meant to say was, how great it is, the three of us here in this land of opportunity that's Ireland. And before you say any more, don't forget it was me who persuaded you to take this job.'

She laughed.

'True!'

'So friends?'

'Friends!'

She leaned forward and kissed him on the cheek.

Jonas entered the restaurant.

'Watch out!' Simon said under his breath. 'You know how jealous he is!'

She turned towards the door and waved Jonas over.

'I called my father last night,' she said as Jonas sat down. 'He's got a gig Sunday week in Dalkey. Fancy going?'

'Sure.'

'I'll get him to reserve tickets.'

———

On Saturday she rode into Dublin, crossing the Liffey at Ellis Quay, and made her way via Manor Street to a small cluster of single-storey workers cottages, built in the traditional Irish style. The cottages were a left-over from the early days of the city's industrialisation and it was a wonder they'd escaped developers. Though her father complained of gentrification, it didn't look much like it to her. The kids on the street were typically rough and as she removed her helmet she heard a woman shouting and the front door of a house was flung open. A dishevelled-looking man stumbled out, muttering furiously to himself, and set off down the street. The drunks, it seemed, hadn't changed much either.

Fela went over to two teenagers seated on a wall, smoking.

'Keep an eye on my bike? I'll not be long.'

She opened her palm to reveal two euro coins then pocketed them.

The boys nodded. She crossed the street and rang her father's bell.

The man who opened the door was tall and slightly stooped, with eyes of still startling blue. He had a couple of days' growth of beard, hair striped like a badger and tied back in a pony tail. He spread his arms wide to welcome his daughter.

'How's my gorgeous girl?' He pulled her close, crushing her cheek against his own bristly one. 'Come on in. Kettle's on and there's whisky in the jar!'

'Don't give me that old Oirish routine, Da!'

He laughed as he followed her into the house.

Inside she looked around at the neat living room.

'What's happened?'

'Had a bit of a tidy up, threw some things away. Should have done it years ago.'

'So what brought this on?'

He shrugged. 'I don't want to leave a load of junk for you to sort out.'

'Why, are you going somewhere?'

'I'm thinking of selling up. Property prices have gone crazy round here and I might as well cash in while the going's good.'

'But this place is your home!'

'I come here less and less often, and when I do there's building work going on over by the old barracks and lorries thundering past day and night. A development company bought up the whole Murray estate.'

'D'you know what they're planning to do with it?'

'Pull down most of these buildings and redevelop, I guess. But if they do there'll have to be compensation... I'll fetch the tea. It's all ready.'

'At least wait for their offer.'

She took a seat on the saggy leather sofa, covered by a bright rug hand-crocheted by her grandmother. She felt a deep attachment to the place, so full of memories. When she was small her mother had come too but after they split up she'd put her into the hands of some kindly stranger for the ferry crossing, to be met by him on the other side. On Fridays she'd fetch the eggs for their tea from a woman a few doors down who kept chickens in her back yard. She'd reach into the nesting box and feel the downy warmth of the hen's bottom then carefully extract the precious booty. No egg ever tasted as good or had as velvety a yolk as 'her' eggs.

Her father returned with a tray, two mugs of tea and a fruit cake.

'Mrs Galt's been baking. If I eat this thing by myself, my cholesterol'll go through the roof.'

'Give some to the neighbours.'

'I'd never hear the end of it. She calls them thieving tinkers.'

'Okay, I'll take some to Jonas. He loves homemade cake. Reminds him of his amah in Matjiesfontein.'

'Was she a baker?'

'She did everything. They wouldn't have survived without her.'

She cut herself a large slice.

'So how's the job going in that shiny new city of Mammon?'

'They don't all have horns and cloven hooves.'

'So you're enjoying yourself?'

'It's a challenge. I like that.'

'You always did! You'll end up ruling the world!'

'In your dreams, Da! But I'm enjoying learning new things. My boss encourages me to be enterprising. Not something I'm used to.'

'You like him?'

'I'm not sure. He's intelligent.'

'Your mother valued intelligence above all else. Myself, I favour the creative spirit.'

'Don't they go together?'

'Not always. Intelligence can block instinct, which is where creativity comes from.'

'But it needs intelligence to shape it.'

Sean sighed. 'You'd make a good lawyer! Like your Ma!'

'You loved her, didn't you?'

'She was the love of my life... Which didn't mean we could stall together.'

'I know.'

For a brief moment both were silent.

'Are you bringing those two friends of yours to the gig Sunday?'

'Yes. We'd like to buy you dinner afterwards.'

'That'd be grand. But you need to book. Weekends in Dalkey are madness.'

He stood up, went over to the bureau and opened a drawer. 'I found these during my tidy up. I thought you might like them.'

He handed her a large brown envelope. Inside were photos, some in colour, some black and white. She picked out one or two at random. One showed her father, young and handsome with curly dark hair, another her Irish grandmother, white haired but still tall and strong, and herself aged around four holding her grandma's hand against a background of the mountains of Mayo. She felt a sudden pang of nostalgia for that half-forgotten landscape of childhood.

'You're sure you want to part with them, Da?'

'They're just lying there in the drawer.'

She pulled out another. A dark-skinned young woman with braided hair and a smile that lit up her face, stood in a garden holding a lighter skinned child in her arms. At the sight of her mother, tears gathered unbidden in her eyes. Quickly she turned back to the picture of her grandmother.

'Gran used to call me her little picaninny! Not a word you can say any more... When did she die?'

'Two years ago. Ninety-six and still going strong. She always asked after you.'

She should have made the effort to visit more often but

it was too late now. Living in England, Ireland had seemed such a world away.

'I was up there a couple of days ago and took a peek into that great hangar your people have put up there.'

'A research base?'

He nodded.

'They've notices up all over the place saying, "Private Property. Keep Out."'

'So you were trespassing.'

'I was walking your grandma's dog the neighbours are looking after. He took off over the wall into the estate and when he refused to come back I had to get him. Eventually I found a break in one of the electric fences, a poacher's run, well hidden. Anyway by the time I caught up with him, he'd nipped into the hangar they've got there through a side door. I grabbed him just as he was lifting his leg against one of their precious plants.'

He grinned mischievously.

'Did anyone see you?'

'Not as far as I know.'

'What was in there?'

'Plants, as far as the eye could see. And great arc lights beaming down. Then along one of the rows came a small girl I know from the village with a watering can in her hands, watering the plants. She said they were thirsty.'

'That must have been quite a job!'

'They did look a bit dried up. I told her she'd be in trouble for trespassing and I'd see her home. Then the sprinklers came on and there was something in the air that made you cough.'

'Why are you telling me this?'

'It's the same throughout the world, companies like yours taking over. Even Mayo's not safe from their grasp.'

'It's just research, Da, to improve crop yields. With all the drought now, poor farmers need these improvements.'

'Poison, more like! Now they're poisoning the fish in the sea!'

'Not all research is harmful. Some even makes things better.'

He sighed. 'You're right. I'm just an old dinosaur.'

Despite her father's gloom, she left the house feeling light-hearted as she always did after spending time with him. He was incapable of staying down for long, though his tidying up and offer of photographs made her uneasy, as if he were tying up the loose ends of his life.

Out on the street the boys had disappeared but her bike was still there.

————

During the following week Fela concentrated on mastering the demands of her new job. Conrad treated her inexperience with commendable patience, though when in a fit of frustration she lost her temper and banged her hands down on the keyboard, he walked out and left her to it. When he returned after a couple of hours to continue their work, he dismissed her attempts at apology for her childish behaviour and merely asked if she was ready to get back to work.

Most of the time she was quick to grasp what was needed, but by the end of the day she was exhausted and wanted only to go home, eat a sandwich with a glass of wine and get into bed. Jonas asked if something was wrong but she told him her unsociability was merely temporary while she learned the ropes of her new job, and that they'd see each other at the weekend. Simon said nothing. He knew well her competitive spirit and that she would not rest until her competence was no longer in doubt.

———

On Saturday Simon and Jonas picked her up in the second-hand VW Jonas had bought and they drove to Dalkey in good time for the gig. It was in a bar down by the harbour and cars were parked along the street for several hundred yards in both directions so it was hard to find a space.

Inside, the bar was packed. Members of the band wandered around a small stage, checking leads and sound levels. There were five of them, percussion, keyboard, two guitar players, and Sean on fiddle. He and the bass guitar also sang vocals. They turned down the massive speakers, claiming they distorted sound and destroyed the sense of intimacy that was the hallmark of the band.

Fela found a table in the corner, while Simon and Jonas went to the bar to order drinks. She loved the busyness before a gig, wires being unravelled and connections checked, short bursts of drumbeat and the occasional shriek of feedback from a mic. Despite most of them being in their sixties the band had lost none of their popularity. Some fans attended every gig and had travelled miles to be in the company of their heroes. Eventually the chatter gave way to an air of expectation as the musicians settled into their places, and a moment later they took off in a burst of sound.

As they got into their stride her father's fiddling grew more and more frenzied. Jonas leaned across to her.

'Your Dad's still got what it takes!'

She nodded, excited. 'Soon he'll have them up and dancing!'

During the next number several members of the audience did indeed rise to their feet and others quickly followed. Those who couldn't find a space sat drumming their heels and swaying their bodies to the rhythm. Simon leapt up and, reaching for Fela's hands, pushed their way into the melee.

The room was growing hotter as one tune followed another with scarcely a pause for breath. Then, suddenly, the music slurred to a halt. It took a moment to register the silence. Fela stopped dancing and gazed around her in confusion but could see nothing through the crush of still gyrating bodies. She heard someone shout for a doctor and, fearful now, began to elbow her way through the clamouring people to the stage. As she came closer she could see a body collapsed on the ground. One of the musicians recognised her and called out, 'Make way!' He leaned down and, grabbing her hand, pulled her onto the stage.

Her father was stretched out awkwardly on the dusty boards fighting for breath. The bass guitarist picked up his violin from the floor and stood holding it, uncertain what to do next. Another of the musicians was kneeling over him. Fela knelt down on his other side. His face was flushed and the rasping sound of his breathing was horrible. Panic stricken, she stroked his brow. It felt cold and damp.

An ambulance arrived and she and two band members accompanied Sean the short drive to St Michael's Hospital. Simon and Jonas were to follow by car. Inside the ambulance the paramedics fitted an oxygen mask but by the time they arrived Sean had lost consciousness.

For almost an hour Fela sat waiting in the corridor. Eventually she ordered Simon and Jonas to go home, saying she'd call them in the morning with any news. She wanted to be alone with her father when they let her into his room.

When at last she was allowed in, he appeared to be asleep. She pulled up a chair to his bedside, and took the hand that lay inert on the white sheet. For hours she sat vigil, paralysed by the nausea of fear. The warmth of her father's fingers in hers was the only thing that gave sign of life or hope that at any moment he might open his eyes.

She must have dozed off because she came to with a start when suddenly his breathing grew loud and laboured, then stopped altogether. She rang the bell frantically and a nurse bustled in, examined the readings on the machine Sean was wired up to then rang for the medical team. They arrived within seconds and one of the nurses escorted her out and asked her to wait. She obeyed meekly, overcome by terror.

In the corridor she paced up and down, unable to stay still. One minute it was impossible to believe anything disastrous could have befallen the man who only hours ago she'd seen fiddling for his very life. The next she understood with sickening certainty that he was dying.

Through the window at the end of the corridor the flashing blue lights of an ambulance punctuated the misty grey dawn. The world was coming awake. Footsteps approached along the corridor and she turned to see a young doctor. For a moment, pity for his exhaustion after a long night of duty almost obscured her fear. He cleared his throat and placed a hand on her arm, drawing her down onto a nearby bench.

'I've bad news, I'm afraid.'

He paused and took her hand. 'Your father's heart has stopped beating and we've been unable to restart it. In a short while the machines will be switched off... Your father is dead.'

She gazed at him in silence, trying to make sense of his words. Eventually she said, 'Can I see him?'

The doctor nodded.

———

F ela emerged from the hospital into a chill mist that blew in from the sea. Jonas was waiting at the wheel of his car with Simon in the passenger seat. Seeing her approach, Simon got out, hurried over and wrapped her shivering body in his coat. She was still dressed in her clothes from the previous evening. He helped her into the back seat and got in beside her, holding her tight against him. For a while none of them spoke.

At length Jonas said, 'D'you want to go home? Or somewhere else? Just say.'

She shook her head. 'It doesn't matter. He's gone! All his laughter and stories and music! There's nothing but a great gaping hole!'

———

Sunday passed somehow. They drove down the coast then took a walk along the drizzly shore. Returning to Jonas's and Simon's flat they bought fresh bread from a Moroccan bakery and Jonas made soup. Fela ate, unaware of what she was eating. In the afternoon Simon put on an old black and white film and she fell asleep on the sofa. When she woke the film was over and she said she wanted to go home.

Jonas drove her. Her landlady, Mrs Docherty, who'd heard of Sean's death in a radio news bulletin, met them on the doorstep. Dismissing Jonas gently but firmly, she insisted on taking charge. She saw Fela into bed, brought her hot whisky, and sat beside her as she fell into a troubled sleep.

At seven she woke as usual, got out of bed, showered and did her best to disguise with makeup the marks of grieving. The last thing she wanted was to sit at home brooding, despite the kindly attentions of Mrs Docherty.

Conrad was surprised when she entered his office. With uncharacteristic spontaneity he went up to her and took her hands in his.

'I didn't think you'd be in today. You mustn't feel any pressure to return until you're ready.'

'Thanks, but I'd rather be here.'

He released her and turned back to his desk.

'Your father was one of the finest fiddlers in Ireland, maybe the world. I'm a big fan of his music.'

'Really? I wouldn't put you down as a fan of traditional Irish music. More Mozart, or jazz.'

'I've got all his recordings. CD, vinyl, and several gigs I've taped myself. I can lend them to you, if you'd like.'

'Thanks, I'd appreciate that.'

His enthusiasm was making her emotional and she moved the conversation onto more neutral ground.

'How did you come across him?'

'Joburg. He and his band were part of the celebrations at the end of apartheid. They were always great favourites with the Africans.'

She nodded.

'He met my mother in Joburg and went back whenever he could. How come you were there?'

'Taking a break from my duties. I was a soldier. After the gig, we all went on to celebrate – possibly your mother too. It was an unforgettable night!'

A soldier! It made sense – something in his physical bearing. Experience in the army was probably considered an asset in business these days, she thought grudgingly.

'When did you leave the army?'

'Eight years ago. I'd already decided studying was better than fighting, and the army will pay.'

It was a relief to talk about someone else, and she was genuinely curious.

'So what did you do next?'

'When I joined up I was more or less illiterate. Then I discovered a taste for books.'

'Not a life that encourages reading, I'd have thought.'

'Like anything else, it has its longeurs. A book's useful to fill the time.'

'I guess so.'

She turned to return to her room.

'Let me know when you'd like to hear your father's recordings. And feel free to make your own hours for the rest of the week.'

———

It was Friday evening, the end of a difficult week for Simon and Jonas, doing their best to comfort Fela without crowding her. Simon tried to get her to talk, with small success. Remembering, it seemed, was too painful and she found refuge in a kind of willed amnesia. She arranged to see her new friend Maeve at the small restaurant she ran near the harbour in Dún Laoghaire, and tired of the limits of the Industrial Village, Jonas suggested he and Simon take a trip into town.

With a slightly guilty sense of liberation they sauntered along Pearse St., pausing in front of the thick plate glass window of an expensive car dealer where a glossy Mercedes revolved on its plinth under an artfully arranged spotlight.

'Look at that beauty!' Jonas said.

'I prefer the 4 by 4 over there. Only 20,000 on the clock.'

'What is it you don't appreciate about modern design? You're a scientist but you're like some old hippie!'

'I just don't share your enthusiasm for material goods.'

'So what is it that turns you on?'

Simon shrugged.

'I wish I knew.'

Jonas shook his head but said no more. He wasn't in the mood for deep conversation.

'Anyway neither of us should be buying anything right now,' Simon continued. 'Rumour has it we may all be out of a job in a few months, unless we're prepared to move to Africa or wherever the company decides to relocate its R and D.'

'When did you hear that?'

'Weiss is back from Geneva. He had me into his office this morning. The Swiss bosses are worried about the precarious state of the Irish economy and say we need to up our productivity. They want to see a significant return on their investment, and soon.'

'I've just completed the trials on the fertiliser. That should satisfy them for a while.'

'Yes, Weiss is touting it as the answer to third-world drought. It seems you're up for a prize.'

'And your vaccine? You told him you're having problems?'

Simon groaned. 'For what it was worth! He doesn't listen and wants everything yesterday.'

'That's commerce for you!'

Jonas waved at the salesman to get his attention.

'What about taking that Merc for a test drive?'

———

I n the bedroom of a small cottage in a village in Mayo, a woman sat beside her sick child. Every now and then she reached down to mop the little girl's brow with a clean flannel. She was small for her ten years and restless with fever. She pushed aside the thick quilt on her parents' double bed as the door opened and a tall man entered the room, pulling the door quietly to behind him.

'The doctor's on his way. How's she doing?'

They spoke in Irish.

'Listen to her breathing!'

The woman's eyes never left the child, whose laboured breaths filled the quiet room.

'I'll rest with you till he comes.'

He laid a hand on the woman's shoulder as she raised her face to him.

'Aren't you needed at the plantation?'

'I put the sprinklers on. They'll not miss me for a couple of hours.'

He pulled up a chair to join her at her vigil but said nothing about the news he'd just heard over the radio of the sudden death of the famous musician, Sean O'Connor, son of this parish.

———

T he conference hall in the company HQ was rapidly filling up. Company top brass, as well as luminaries from Dublin's banking and business world, a handful of academics, and a representative from the Ministry for

Business, Enterprise and Innovation had all arrived for Associated Swiss Pharmaceuticals' annual prize giving for the most promising new research.

Estelle Lanvier, a handsome woman of around fifty, recently appointed Professor of Biochemistry at University College Dublin, was amongst the invited guests. Her severe black suit was embellished by crystals, sewn onto its collar and cuffs that gave off sparks of light as she moved. Her glossy black hair was twisted into a coil at the back of her head, which with her antique silver earrings gave her a Spanish air. She glanced over the shoulder of the man she was talking to and observed Conrad Dreyer enter by a side door. Excusing herself, she made her way through the crowd towards him.

He greeted her with a look of pleased surprise as she kissed him on both cheeks.

'Congratulations! I hear this year's prize winner's one of your latest recruits,' she said.

'Yes, he's been with us a little over three months. I just found out you were in Dublin.'

'We'd have run into one another sooner or later.'

She looked around to where Jonas was standing talking to Weiss and a representative from the Swiss parent company.

'Another of your latest protégés, Simon Eastlake, is an ex-Ph.D student of mine. Quite a coincidence, wouldn't you say?'

'Serendipity! Or is it synchronicity? He's working on something pretty interesting too.'

'And what exactly would that be?'

'It's early days.'

She smiled.

'Dear Conrad! Always keep your cards close to your chest! Simon's brilliant but a bit of a maverick.'

'Often the case with the brightest. I better go and do my duty. See you later for a drink?'

'If you're not too caught up.'

She glanced around the room.

'Seems the whole Politburo's here!'

'A lot's riding on these young men.'

She nodded.

'Indeed! I hear the company's in need of a profitable new line.'

He smiled but said nothing.

'You'd better go!'

Despite his formal dress, she thought how he radiated a different kind of energy as he approached a group of men in evening suits, standing near the podium. It must be eight years since they'd last met and she wondered if he found her much changed.

Fela pushed her way through the crowd to where Simon was standing alone against the wall. His expression showed he was in no mood for festivities, and neither was she. But it would have been churlish to miss Jonas's big night.

'What's up?'

'I hate these occasions.'

'If I didn't know you better I'd say you were jealous,' she said to lighten the tone.

'Of Jonas?' He snorted. 'What I hate is the whole thing turned into a publicity stunt, just so bigwigs and business people can feel good about themselves.'

'Their support's needed. Anyway Jonas deserves his moment of glory. What he's done will help transform food production in developing countries.'

'Single handed!'

'Don't be mean.'

'You're right!' He made a gesture of contrition. 'But don't ask me to join in.'

The ceremony was about to begin. She left Simon and moved forward to get a better view of the stage, in the crush almost treading on the elegantly shod toes of a tall, well-built woman in a black suit. Dr Weiss and Conrad ascended the podium, beside which Jonas was waiting to be called up. He looked very smart in his suit and striped shirt, his fine dark hair newly trimmed. She'd never thought of him as handsome, being rather too slight and sharp featured for her taste. But success gave him a newfound confidence.

Weiss stepped to the microphone. 'Ladies, Gentlemen and Distinguished Guests, I'd like to welcome you all on the occasion of our annual award for the most innovative research of 2008. This fertiliser will be of huge benefit to struggling farmers all over the world, especially those in the most deprived areas. So our annual prize goes to Dr Jonas Finzi, with the additional mention of Dr. James Lydon, who unfortunately can't be with us tonight.'

There was a burst of applause as Jonas ascended the steps to the platform, where Weiss was holding out a small bronze statue of a man in a lab coat bending over a microscope.

'Thank you, sir! I'm deeply honoured to receive this, not just for myself but especially on behalf of my predecessor, Dr James Lydon, who deserves it even more than me.'

Another burst of applause from the crowd.

After the speeches were concluded, the guests shuffled into the neighbouring room, where drinks and a buffet had been laid out. Fela followed. Simon seemed to have disappeared but Conrad was standing just inside the doorway next to Jonas and the dark-haired woman Fela had almost trodden on. Fela was about to turn away when Conrad spotted her and called her over.

'This is Estelle Lanvier, Professor of Biochemistry at UC. My assistant, Felicity O'Connor.'

'Fela, please! We've not met, but I've heard about you from my friend Simon Eastlake. You were his tutor at Uni,' Fela said, offering her hand to Estelle's firm grasp.

'Ah ha!.. So tell me, is that Fela as in Fela Kuti? I'm a great admirer of his music.'

'Just a coincidence, I'm afraid.'

She felt herself blushing. There was something condescending in Estelle's tone that made her hackles rise.

Estelle gestured to include Jonas. 'And now all three of you are here at ASP. Simon used to refer to you as The Three Musketeers!'

'That might describe him. I'm not so sure about Fela and me,' Jonas replied, laughing.

Estelle smiled. 'You must have many people to speak to, and I too had better circulate... It's nice to meet you,' she said to Fela. Then to Conrad, 'Call me when you have a moment.'

Fela observed her as she moved away.

'You never met Dr. Lanvier at Newcastle?' Conrad said, following her gaze.

She shook her head. 'How do you know her?'

She was asking out of politeness, not really interested in the answer.

'Oh, we go back a long way. Our paths haven't crossed for a while.'

'I'll leave you to your duties. See you on Monday.'

Eager to make her escape, she pushed her way through the crowd towards the exit.

———

Conrad was seated in front of his computer. The reception was over, people had left, and the building was dark except for security lights. His attention was caught by something in the grainy surveillance footage on his screen. He leaned forward to take a closer look. It showed the inside of a hangar at the Mayo plantation, where a man, who on closer inspection he recognised to his astonishment as Sean O'Connor, was bending over a little girl holding a watering can. A moment later from a different camera a figure in protective clothing and wearing a mask entered the hangar, turned a tap attached to the wall and a fine mist began to rain down from the sprinklers. Conrad cut back to the first camera and froze the image, gazing intently at the screen. As he released it, he saw Sean picked up the girl and hurried out of shot. Conrad got up and walked over to the window. He gazed out at the fading outline of distant hills.

The phone rang. He returned to the desk and picked up the receiver.

'Conrad? It's Simon. I need to talk to you.'

'Tomorrow first thing in my office.'

'I'd rather meet somewhere else. Now, if possible.'

Conrad paused.

'Where are you?'

'Round the corner. Logan's Bar.'

'Okay, I'll be there in ten.'

He sighed as he replaced the receiver. Weiss had already cornered him as he was leaving the ceremony, concerned about Simon's progress with the vaccine. No doubt he'd also been pressuring him, as if Jonas's success wasn't enough to be going on with.

He returned to the computer, copied the CCTV footage from the plantation onto a USB stick, deleted it then shut down.

———

The bar was a new one, situated on the ground floor of one of the gleaming high-rise buildings that made up Dublin's rapidly expanding business quarter. Simon was seated at a table near the window half way through a pint of Guinness. Conrad ordered another from the bar and went over to join him.

'Couldn't this wait until tomorrow?' he said as he sat down.

'I don't think so… It seems the company's got financial worries.'

'Is that what you wanted to talk about?"

'Dr Weiss called me to his office yesterday. He made it clear he's relying on the rotavaccine I'm working on to secure the company's future in Ireland. Compared to the big players we're small potatoes and, according to him, without it we may not weather the current financial storm.'

The barman came over and placed the Guinness in front of Conrad, who nodded his thanks.

'What else did he say?'

He didn't know Simon well but sensed any attempt to bully him would prove counterproductive.

'He's flying out to South America next week to discuss a deal.'

'I believe he is.'

'But the vaccine isn't fully tested.'

'No doubt he's just feeling the ground.'

'He can do that over the internet.'

'These things are best done face to face.'

'Guatemala's known for not requiring the usual government controls. They sell stuff on, no questions asked and none of the usual guarantees. It's a well-known method of testing a product before introducing it to more lucrative Western markets.'

'Weiss wouldn't be party to that sort of thing.'

'No? I believe he plans to do just that.'

'Our reputation's too important.'

'It may be technically illegal but pharma companies all over the world use third parties for such deals.'

'I assure you there is no deal. I've told him we need another six months to complete initial trials. With the success of the fertiliser, he agreed to that.'

'It will still need proper monitoring in the right conditions. We can't be rushed. The risks are too great, especially in the case of children with different immunity levels in the developed world, where the drug's ultimately headed. What may not harm a Ugandan child can kill an American. Tell him when it's ready he'll have a product that will earn him a fortune, but not yet.'

'Your predecessor, Dr Murphy, told him we were almost there. What's gone wrong?'

'It seems his latest trial revealed potentially dangerous side effects he's been unable to counteract. That's the reason he quit.'

Simon laid a hand-written piece of paper on the table and pushed it towards Conrad.

'Where did you get this?'

'Read it. It was in the files. He found evidence that vaccinated children have a three times greater risk of suffering from intestinal bleeding and other complications.'

'If this is true, why hasn't it been made known?'

'Ask Weiss. He'd surely have been informed.'

Conrad read over Murphy's notes carefully then looked up.

'Weiss is claiming it as a major breakthrough against the most prevalent strains of the disease. It's a big deal for the company.'

'If he has any concern for our reputation, let alone any conscience, he must know it's far too soon to go public. It seems Murphy got wind of his intention and that's the reason he quit.'

'He said he was leaving because of family problems.'

Simon shrugged.

'Okay, I'll talk to Weiss. But the company owns the research, Simon, not you. They can replace you with someone more compliant any time they want.'

'If that's their decision, it'll be their shame. And I won't go quietly.'

'You may be a scientist but you're working in the cut-throat world of commerce. From their point of view even if there are harmful side effects how long before the world gets to know about it? Ten years, twenty before the law suits start coming in? You have to give me a clearer idea of how long you need to put things right, the shortest time possible. I'll do my best to get them to listen but there's no guarantee I'll succeed.'

Simon's face was flushed with anger.

'I'm ready to go through the results so far with whoever wants to see them.'

Conrad gave a snort of exasperation.

'They're not interested in scientific details, Simon. Any more than the shareholders! They want a product.'

Simon swallowed his beer and stood up.

'Tell them science dictates profit, not the other way around! I'll be in the lab when you need me.'

Conrad watched as he strode to the door and disappeared onto the street. He got up, went over to the bar and ordered a double Jameson's. Simon might be an infuriating pain in the arse but what he said couldn't just be pushed aside. On the other hand, for a middle-ranking manager to take on the might of ASP would be embarking on a fight he had small chance of winning. For now all he wanted was to get drunk.

———

Jonas was not yet back when Simon returned to the flat. He took off his jacket, chucked it over the back of the sofa, and switched on the TV. The flickering images with the sound turned to a subliminal buzz made the silence less loud and left his thoughts free. Watching Jonas receive his prize had disturbed him deeply. It wasn't that he was jealous, as Fela had claimed. It was registering the seductive effect of success, even on those who believed themselves immune. It led with horrible inevitability to the erosion of moral scruples and a willingness to play with people's lives.

The downstairs door buzzer went. He cursed under his breath and decided to ignore it. It came again, more insistent. Whoever it was wasn't going away. He went over to the intercom.

'Let me in,' Fela demanded.

'Can't it wait till tomorrow? I'm beat.'

'Come on, Simon! I won't stay long.'

He opened the door and leaving it ajar, went into the kitchen to see if there was anything for supper. A couple of minutes later Fela entered, out of breath from the stairs.

'Bloody lift's stuck and the building's brand new!'

'People jam the doors when they're bringing up a load of stuff.'

She flopped down on a chair.

'Where's Jonas?'

Simon shrugged.

'Celebrating, no doubt… Is there a reason for this visit or are you just looking for company?'

She pulled a letter out of her pocket and laid it on the worktop.

'This came from the hospital. They say they're not doing an autopsy on my Da.'

'Were you expecting one?'

'They're claiming his death was due to an asthma attack. He never had asthma in his life.'

'He smoked, didn't he? And people can develop asthma at any age.'

'He gave up smoking five years ago.'

'That means little. You know that.'

He took eggs and a pack of mushrooms out of the fridge and set about cracking the eggs into a bowl.

'I'm making omelettes. Want one?'

'I'm not hungry.'

Simon sliced some mushrooms and tipped them with a slurp of oil into a frying pan.

'If they won't change their minds I'll pay someone.'

'And what good will that do? I know what a shock his death is and how much he meant to you. But I don't see how this will help.'

'I don't believe it was natural causes.'

'You mean someone killed him! '

'Or some thing.'

'Come on, Fela! He'd had a stroke and he drank too much. This is grief talking, not your rational self.'

'You didn't sit with him that last night. It was like his whole system had packed up. Not just an asthma attack.' She paused. 'He'd just come back from visiting his home village, near the research plantation. I saw some CCTV footage on Conrad's computer and I was curious so I ran it. Sean was in the hangar, and a child.'

'What does that prove? Maybe you should get some bereavement counselling, someone to help you come to terms with your loss.'

'Oh, please!'

'Honestly, you're wasting your time if the hospital's already given its verdict. It's just the rotten way things turn out. I should know!'

'What does that mean?'

'Some battles are winnable, some aren't.'

Simon began beating the eggs.

'I've been looking up fertiliser production. Phospho-gypsum, for example, is a very effective and a commonly used fertiliser to boost levels of calcium and sulphur in poor soils. It's not permitted above a certain radioactivity level but records of its application rates don't need to be kept, so in fact it can be, and is, used indiscriminately. It can result in systemic failure. Another thing. If such fast acting fertilisers are applied before heavy rainfall, not only do they leach into ground water, poisoning it, but can also under certain conditions give off toxic gas in a confined space. I saw on the CCTV a man in protective clothing turn on the sprinklers.'

'So what d'you want to do? You're a financial assistant, not a scientist. All this is pure speculation.'

'I need to talk to Jonas.'

'And say what? Accuse him of being responsible for your father's death? Don't you think you need a bit more evidence before doing a thing like that?'

She sat down on a stool and covered her face with her hands.

'Everything looked so rosy. Good jobs, good money, the life we'd dreamed of.'

She began to weep. Simon turned off the gas and took her in his arms. Perhaps if she cried enough she'd exhaust herself, then he could lay her down in the spare room and let her sleep.

———

She sleepwalked through the days up to her father's funeral. She'd handed over the arrangements to members of his band, who having worked together for so many years seemed more qualified to give him the send-off he'd have wished. They decided on a 'green' funeral, to be held at the Woodbrook natural burial ground near Wexford, a grave set in a meadow of tall grasses, cowslips, wild anemones, and young saplings. Musicians came from all over Ireland, a young priest blessed the grave and the band played a medley of Sean's favourite songs. After that everyone made for the nearest bar. Fela went too but stayed only briefly. It was too noisy and there were too many people, though everyone welcomed her warmly, talking lovingly of her father. The ceremony had been as joyful as any such occasion could be and Sean would have been all set to make a night of it. But she was exhausted and needed to go home.

———

The following day Conrad stood in their communicating doorway, observing her as she cursed aloud at a calculation error she'd made in her spreadsheet.

'You need to take a few days off. You're in no fit state to work.'

She looked up. Grief made her delicate face peaky and there were dark rings under her eyes.

'I'm just tired. I'm not sleeping.'

'You've just buried your Dad. There's no good trying to carry on as usual.'

'When I'm not working I get time to think and that's worse.'

'Take your bike and see a bit of the country while the weather holds. Nothing lifts the spirits like riding the empty roads and discovering new places.'

'Maybe.'

'Take the rest of the week and see how you feel on Monday.'

His expression had lost its natural severity and in her vulnerable state she was susceptible to the least sign of sympathy. Perhaps a few days travelling around the country was a good idea.

———

Back home she stuffed a few things into a bag, together with a map of Ireland. She would ride west till she reached her grandmother's village. She had clear memories of her cottage, where her father had grown up with two sisters, living now in America with families of their own. Amongst the snapshots Sean had given her was one of herself aged around four, helping her grandmother to plant nasturtiums in the front garden. She could remember the photo being taken, though sometimes it was hard to tell what were her own recollections and what were repetitions of others that had assumed the status of memory.

She decided to take the road via Athlone to Galway, then on to Connemara through Joyce Country to Clew Bay. For the first part of the journey she rode as fast as she could, given the narrow roads and procession of heavy farm vehicles. Athlone was a dreary town and it was impossible to find a cup of decent coffee, so she bought a sandwich and a bottle of water and kept moving.

By the time she reached Galway it was growing dark. The city was full of life after the depressing towns of the Midlands. The streets were crowded with people, most of them young, and music poured out of every heaving bar. The docks were still more animated, nothing like the forlorn, half-derelict place her father had once inhabited. Ireland's newfound prosperity seemed to have swept all before it, including the ancient goat who'd dwelt in the car park, with his filthy dreadlocks, yellow devil's eyes and ripe stench.

She came to a square near the centre of town, where a group of drunken vagrants and some children were camped out on a square of trampled grass, and another recollection sprang to life – a woman singing as men argued and fought, the rank smell of booze and someone yelling at a barking dog. Above all she remembered the feeling of fear as she begged her father to carry her through the drunken throng, and him telling her not to be a cry baby. She'd shouted at him that she wanted to go home, and he'd said this was home, until her sobs forced him to relent and they returned to the squat where he was shacked up. She revved up the bike and took off in another direction.

She found a B and B at the edge of town, where she fell asleep almost at once. In the morning she was up and breakfasted by nine. As she drove over the causeway into Connemara, she raised her visor and drew in deep breaths of clean salt air. With the engine slowed to a soft purr, she could hear the cries of curlews and the distant sound of the waves, or perhaps it was only the wind sighing through scrubby trees at the field's edge. At the next junction she turned inland towards Oughterard and a distant line of purple hills, and she felt the tension inside letting go.

Past the far end of the deep inlet known as Killary Harbour, the road turned up into Doo Lough Pass. Once more the sluice gate of memory opened – her father pointing out a stone erected at the roadside to mark the men, women and children who'd perished there during the Great Famine. There were tears in his eyes as he made her stand and listen for the keening of their ghosts. She'd heard nothing except the wind that gusted over the wild empty land beneath a sky shredded with blown clouds he'd called mares' tails.

A few miles further on she turned again towards the coast in the direction of her father's village. Tall wrought-iron gates came into view, from which an avenue led up to a great house, half-obscured by trees. A notice was fixed to the gates: Warning, Trespassers Keep Out. Property of Associated Swiss Pharmaceuticals Ltd.

She pulled up to take a better look. Ever since she'd known it, the place had been abandoned, its gates sagging on their hinges so that it was easy to squeeze through and play hide and seek in the overgrown garden. Now the hinges were mended and the gates securely locked, under the all-seeing eye of a CCTV camera. She stared at the notice. It seemed a strange coincidence that this old property, so far from Dublin, should have been bought by the very company she worked for.

She set off again and reaching the village, drove slowly along the main street. The bar, which was also a shop, now sported a B and B sign in the window. Further on the buildings petered out, and the road turned into a single track leading down to a small harbour. Her grandmother's house was at the head of the track, a single-storey cottage, whitewashed with a corrugated iron roof that had replaced the original thatch. The small front garden, once full of flowers and patterns lovingly created out of shells and stones gathered from the strand, was now a bare strip of unkempt ground. It was getting dark, and there were no lights or any sign of habitation. Her father had talked of selling, but as far as she knew nothing had come of it. Often he left a key with someone in the village. She decided to ask at the bar.

The bar was separated from the shop by a narrow corridor. When she entered, a woman in the shop part was filling up the shelves and turned to greet her.

'Was it you I heard riding up on that great beast of a machine?' she said. 'You'll be the talk of the town surely!'

'It was. I wonder if you can help me?'

'Ask away.'

'My father, Sean O'Connor, lived at the white cottage at the end of the village. I'm wondering if he left a key with anyone.'

'He did so.'

She went behind the counter, opened a small cupboard to reveal a row of keys with faded labels hung on hooks, selected one and handed it to Fela. 'You'll be Sean's daughter? How is our man? Still playing his fiddle like the very devil?'

'My father died unexpectedly.'

The woman's face fell. 'I'm sorry to hear that now! It's not long he was here. The weather was bad, so he slept in one of the rooms upstairs rather than in that cold cottage. Whatever happened, if you'll forgive me for asking?'

'The hospital said an asthma attack. We don't rightly know.'

'You poor girl, losing your da like that! That's shocking news, indeed it is!'

The woman's distress was obvious and Fela bit back her own emotion.

'Thanks for the keys. I'll return them when I leave.'

'You'll not find the place very welcoming. It hasn't been lived in for a while and it'll be damp and cold. You'd better come here for your meal, and there's a warm bed if you want it.'

'I'll remember that.'

The woman smiled and returned to her work.

Fela turned the key in the front door of the cottage. The wood had swelled and the door stuck on the flagged floor, so she had to push hard. Inside, the musty smell of damp hit her. The door led straight into the living room. As she switched on the light, she paused for a moment to take in the familiar sights: the rattan lampshade she'd made with her mother's help, and her grandmother's rag rug, originally brightly coloured but faded now, thrown over the back of the sofa where she could still see the hairs of the old dog. In the hearth, the cold remains of a peat fire gave off a faint acrid smell, and the room's unnatural neatness contributed to its air of chill abandon. In the kitchen, a couple of mugs stood on the draining board with the encrusted remains of tea, and the floorcloth draped over the edge of a bucket beside the sink was stiff and dry. She decided not to look into the bedrooms. The woman at the bar was right. The life she remembered had gone out of the place, and it would be impossible to spend the night here. Perhaps in the morning she'd come back and take a better look. For now, all she wanted was to leave.

Back in the bar she ate her supper by the fire, doing her best to ignore the curious stares of a handful of locals. She caught a vestige of the barman's conversation as he explained she'd just lost her father to someone in a hushed voice, and out of respect they left her to herself. As soon as she had eaten, she bid the company goodnight and went upstairs to her room. She lay down on the narrow bed, whose sheets smelt pleasantly of lavender, and gazed out of the dormer window at a sky bright with stars. She thought of her father, her grandmother, and the vanished illusion that coming to Ireland might help her find that elusive sense of identity most people here seemed blessed with. Instead her journey merely underlined that her father's roots were not hers, any more than she was able to share her mother's memories of Jo'burg. She was like some stray mongrel, going from place to place in search of somewhere to call her own.

The following morning she ate a hearty breakfast of ham and eggs in the bar, and fell into conversation with her hostess, whose name was Margaret.

'Did you know my father well?' Fela asked.

'We shared the bus to school each day. There weren't many of us kids, so we had plenty of craic.' She smiled. 'He was a joker, your da. A bit wild but a good heart, and the finest fiddler in Mayo!'

'Did you know that he suffered from asthma?'

'I did not. It's on the rise though. Pollution, they say, from all the chemicals they put into fertilisers and foodstuffs these days.'

'Do you know about anyone in the village being taken ill? A young girl maybe, someone Sean knew?'

The woman thought for a minute. 'There was one, now you mention it. A few weeks back. She was very poorly. She's grand now though.' She crossed herself briefly.

'What happened?'

'No one could account for it. One minute she was on her deathbed, the next, whatever it was gone as quick as it came.'

'Could you tell me the name of the family?'

'Sure. The Fahys. They've the farm next to the big estate.'

'The one that's been bought by the biochemical company?'

'That's the one. The girl's name is Sorcha.'

'Do any of the people who work at the estate come here?'

'Now and then a couple of the workers come by for a drink or a bite to eat. Most are from Dublin. They don't talk much but they're decent enough fellas. It's good to see the old place cared for, not just going to rack and ruin.'

A fter breakfast, Fela walked the mile to the Fahy farm. It wasn't much of a place, just a low stone house with a barn, a muddy yard, some chickens and a dozen ewes in a pen waiting to give birth. She knocked on the door and a young woman opened it. She wore faded blue overalls, and heavy boots with socks rolled down over the tops. Her eyes were the colour of the stormy sea, and her skin pale as porcelain. Her black hair was gathered carelessly into a knot, and she was the most beautiful woman Fela had ever seen.

'Can I help you?' she said hesitantly, as though English wasn't familiar on her tongue.

'My name's Fela O'Connor. I believe you knew my father, Sean? He lived in the village.'

'Sure we know Sean.'

'Did you know he'd been ill?'

'I'm sorry to hear that now.'

'I'm told your little girl was ill too, with breathing problems.'

The woman took a step back, uncertain what this

stranger on her doorstep was after. 'We were worried, that's for sure. But she's back to herself entirely now.'

'That's wonderful. Unfortunately, my father's dead.'

The woman paused. 'I'm very sorry for that…' she repeated, then added, 'Would you care to come in?'

They walked along a chilly passageway but as soon as they entered the flagged kitchen, warmth from the peat fire gave cheer. The room was sparsely furnished but comfortable, with a bright rag rug and an old sofa with cushions covered in squares of coloured knitting. A large deal table was surrounded by six ill-assorted chairs and toys spilled out of a box onto the floor, battered cars, a tractor, Lego pieces and two plastic Barbies, girl and boy. The house was very quiet and there was no sign of children.

The woman poured tea from a large brown pot into a mug, added milk and handed it to Fela, inviting her to sit down.

'Where's your daughter now, if you don't mind me asking?'

'At school. The bus brings her and her brother home around five. Did you want to speak to her?'

She shook her head. 'I'm just wondering if you knew what brought on her illness? If there might be a link between what happened to her and my father?'

'Sean brought her back from the estate. She loves to play there and found her way into the shed with all the plants. She called it her jungle.'

'Did you tell the doctor about this?'

'We didn't think about it at the time. Afterwards, when

she was better, we didn't want her in trouble for trespassing.'

Fela took a sip of her tea. 'So I guess you don't have a report from the doctor?'

The woman shook her head. It was clear Fela's questions were making her uncomfortable.

'Well, at least your daughter's cured now!'

She nodded and crossed herself in a gesture of gratitude.

Fela set down her mug and stood up. 'I better be on my way. Thank you for tea and for talking to me.'

The relief in the woman's face was visible, a woman unused to strangers. At the door she said, 'Your da was a fine man! The best fiddler for miles around!'

'He was indeed!' Fela gazed into the green pools of her eyes in the pale oval of her face, framed by rebellious locks of black hair. Such bewitching beauty called out to be seen and celebrated, not buried in this godforsaken place. Though in her modesty, how she'd have hated that.

———

B ack in Dublin, Fela pulled up in front of Jonas and Simon's apartment block and parked her bike. She walked across the sterile tarmac to the entrance and pressed the intercom for their flat. When there was no immediate answer, she pressed again.

'Okay, Okay! Who is it?' Jonas's voice said.

'Let me in!'

'Fela! What's going on!'

The buzzer went and she entered.

Stepping out of the lift, she saw him waiting for her in his open doorway. 'So what's this? An earthquake?'

'Are you alone? Where's Simon?'

'In his lab. Where else?'

He stood aside for her to enter the flat and closed the door behind them.

'I want to know what's going on at that plantation,' she demanded as soon as the door shut.

'Nice to see you too!'

In the living room someone had obviously been making an effort to make the place more homely. Prints of African landscapes adorned the walls, and a colourful cloth of some traditional design was draped over the beige sofa.

'Improvements, eh?' said Jonas, following her glance.

'I didn't come to discuss the décor. I just need you to tell me what you know about that research base.'

'If you calm down, perhaps you can tell me what you're talking about.'

The flat felt uncomfortably warm after her bike ride. She took off her leather jacket and dropped it on the floor next to her helmet.

'Would you like something to eat or drink?'

She shook her head impatiently. 'I've just come back from Mayo. A child in the village next to the base was ill with breathing problems, like Sean only she survived. It turns out they'd been in the shed where the plants are cultivated. Whatever's going on there's connected to Sean's death. I'm sure of it.'

'Hold on. Those trials are to do with fertilisers and improving water retention for plants in arid places.'

'The child was playing in there, and Sean went to fetch her out.'

'It's a secure area. How did she get in?'

'Obviously not that secure! You know what kids are like. Anyway, whatever's in there killed my father and damn near killed that child as well.'

'You've absolutely no proof of that.'

'It says on his death certificate, he died of an asthma attack. Sean never had asthma in his life! And how come the child also nearly died from severe breathing problems?'

'I've no idea.'

'And you're not suspicious? You could be responsible for the deaths of millions of children in those countries you're selling to!'

'Now hang on! The fertiliser we've developed enables plants to grow stronger and healthier in poor conditions. It's a lifesaver, not a killer. I can't explain what happened to your father, but it's nothing to do with that plantation. D'you think I'd rest for a minute if I thought it had?'

'So why is the place so secret?'

'Because it's a test site! Plants must be grown in carefully controlled conditions that allow us to see how they'll perform in extreme climates. It's just possible that in the confined space of the hangar someone particularly susceptible could be affected during spraying. That's why we take care no unauthorised person enters. In the normal course of things the plants will be grown outdoors.'

'I want an autopsy, not a lecture. Something that says what caused Sean's death.'

'Sean's already buried, Fela,' he said gently.

The anger that had kept her going crumbled and she collapsed onto the sofa. 'So it doesn't matter to you what toxins you're letting loose on the world?'

'It's precisely in order to minimise any such dangers that trials are done. To make sure what we're producing benefits poor farmers and is safe.'

He reached out to take her hand, but she pulled it away.

'Whatever you say, something stinks!'

'Then you'd better not work for pharmaceuticals. Research can't be censored before it gives results, or nothing new would ever be discovered.'

She blew her nose and looked up at him. 'We'll find out for certain when the real trials take place in Africa or wherever you're selling this stuff to, and people start getting sick. But by then it'll be too late.'

'I know how hard it is for you losing your father like that. I'll do anything I can for you, Fela. But I'm not interested in looking for conspiracies where there aren't any. For God's sake, d'you honestly think I'd be party to selling something I knew to be harmful?'

'Knew or just suspected? Without certainty one can persuade oneself of anything!'

She buried her head in her arms. Jonas placed a shawl around her shoulders. 'Get some rest. You're exhausted.'

He tucked the shawl around her then went into the kitchen to make tea.

———

S imon divested himself of gloves and mask and sat down at his computer. He deleted most of the unread emails from a long list, then paused at the most recent, which he read with attention. It was from someone in the Guatemalan Trade Ministry, and addressed to the Dublin CEO of Associated Swiss Pharmaceuticals, Dr Weiss. It had been forwarded to him anonymously, and as he scrolled down he found three other emails from the same source. All dealt with negotiations concerning the sale of his vaccine.

The phone rang. He picked up the receiver.

A voice said, 'Did you get the emails?'

'Estelle? It was you!'

'As soon as you've read them, delete them. We need to talk.'

Simon glanced over at his lab assistant, Paul, who was getting ready to leave.

'D'you mind closing the door after you,' he said over his shoulder.

Paul did so and Simon turned back to the phone.

'Is this evening good?'

'I've got a seminar then I'm meeting someone for dinner. I'll text you with a time and place in the next day or so.'

'I'll be waiting.'

The line went dead and he replaced the receiver. It occurred to him she might have forwarded the emails to Conrad rather than to him. Either she'd already done so, or she didn't want Conrad to know. The thought alarmed him further. But dealing with Estelle was always unpredictable, the antidote to the boredom which Simon was easily prone to. He printed out the emails, then deleted them and switched off his computer. He took off his lab coat, put on his jacket, stuffed the printed emails into his pocket, and locked the lab.

———

I t was the end of the day and the canteen was empty apart from a couple of security staff preparing to take over the night shift, and Conrad. He was sitting near the window drinking coffee, toying with a slice of ginger cake.

Simon went over to his table. 'I went to your office. Fela said I might find you here.'

'So how's it going?'

'Have you seen Weiss?'

'Not today. Why?'

Simon reached into his pocket, pulled out the emails and laid them on the table in front of Conrad.

'I received these.'

Conrad scanned them briefly then looked up. 'Who sent them?'

'I've no idea.'

If Conrad didn't know, Estelle must have her reasons for not including him and he wanted to find out what they were before telling him more.

'It appears the company's gone further with the sale. Trial samples of the vaccine are about to be sent to a South American intermediary, bound no doubt for India or Africa.'

'Has anyone else seen these?'

'No. But if nothing's done, I'll go to the press. It's too late now for negotiation.'

'Hold on. We don't even know if they're genuine.'

'You're saying you know nothing of the deal? You're the head of R and D!'

'Which is what makes me question if they're genuine.'

'They're addressed to the company CEO. In Ireland that's Weiss. Whoever's responsible for setting it up knows exactly how to sell uncertified drugs through a third party.'

Conrad glanced around the canteen for eavesdroppers, but the security guards had left and the woman behind the counter had retreated to the kitchen.

'He's said nothing to me.'

Simon shook his head. 'I warned you. This stuff is going to be used to poison the very people it's intended to help.'

'I've made sure Weiss has Murphy's records, plus the corroborative evidence from recent animal trials. But you're not the only scientist in this field, and they can always replace you.'

'And still he's set on this deal!'

Conrad reached for the emails. 'I assume you have copies.'

Simon didn't but he could no doubt retrieve the originals.

'I can't believe they'd go ahead without consulting you.'

'I'm not lying to you, and it's not illegal.'

'Well, I won't let it happen.'

'Wait a bit. I'll find out what I can.'

Simon stood up. 'And by then it'll be too late!'

S imon returned to his lab in a rage. Conrad maintained he was powerless to prevent the deal even if he wanted to, and he had his doubts about that. It might take months, years even, before any harmful consequences were identified. It was unlikely those would ever be laid at his door, but it was a guilt he wasn't prepared to live with. If scientists kept quiet, there was nothing to prevent those for whom profit was the only concern from ignoring every ethical consideration.

Jonas put his head round the door. 'End of the day, man! I fancy that Thai place for a change.'

'I'm not hungry. I'll join you later for a drink.'

'Okay. Logan's, and don't leave it too long,' said Jonas, shutting the door behind him.

He was in no mood to go drinking with Jonas. He might be his closest friend, but their views differed on a number of things and his present scruples were certain to be one of them. Jonas considered himself a realist, and frequently accused him of seeing things in black and white and refusing to compromise. In turn Simon accused him of lacking the healthy scepticism required by science. Privately he believed Jonas's South African upbringing had something to do with his ability to ignore moral scruples, though he'd never have said so to his face.

Jonas grew up in rural Transvaal during the last years of apartheid. The fear he'd imbibed from birth, coupled with a barely conscious burden of guilt, made him resistant to certain kinds of introspection. In Simon's view it even infected his feelings for Fela, as though being mixed race in some way put her off limits. He knew it was easy for him to make judgements, brought up in Devon by parents who were teachers. In Totnes he'd scarcely encountered a black face, but the moral imperative to fight the vicious scourge of racism had been drummed into him ever since he could remember.

He worked on for almost an hour, looking for anything relating to his research that had passed between Weiss and Head Office. Most of what he found was uninteresting, except one untitled file that was classified and which he was unable to open. It was possible Conrad had the password, in which case Fela might get it for him. It was worth a try.

———

When he entered the bar, the place was still half empty. He ordered a pint of Guinness and brought it to the table, where Jonas was already on his second.

'What I really fancy is a great big bowl of chicken soup with those thick noodles,' Jonas said, as he sat down.

'Okay. Let's finish these and go eat.'

'You look grim. What's wrong?'

'Don't press me.'

He took a long pull of his Guinness. 'The real problem is, I don't know what I'm doing here.'

'Earning a shit load of money and about to get drunk!'

'Yeah, yeah!'

'You've work you enjoy and a good life. All you need is a girlfriend!'

'Thanks!'

'So what then?'

'Research isn't research when the result's already fixed.'

'You want it pure, you become an academic.'

'Even the universities these days are funded by commerce.'

'And he who pays the piper... But even if true independence existed, that wouldn't mean we could control the results. D'you think Einstein foresaw the consequences when he cracked the atom? Science is a risk, so take the money and enjoy the ride!'

Simon gazed gloomily at his half empty glass.

'Listen!' Jonas said. 'Forget the Thai place. Let's pick up Fela and head into town. We all need a night out. We could go to a movie or a club and dance. We could even take a look at that car that took your fancy.'

Simon sighed. 'I suppose if we've sold our souls to Mammon, we might as well enjoy the fruits!'

———

E stelle arrived late at the restaurant where Conrad had been waiting for the past half hour, and was half-way through a bottle of Shiraz. She entered, breathless and apologetic. Not for the first time, he thought what a handsome woman she was. She must be fifty, but there was a vividness about her that defied age.

'So sorry! I was on my way out when I got a call from

Stamford. I'm due to lecture there next month, and what with the nine-hour time gap, I had to take it. Have you ordered?'

He passed her a menu. 'Get your breath back and decide what you want to eat.'

She took off her coat and turned her attention to the menu. The waiter appeared and they ordered, spaghetti vongole for him, vegetarian lasagne for her, a salad to share and another bottle of red.

'So how's things at Dragon's Den?'

Conrad poured her a glass of wine. 'The usual problems when you're managing a team of volatile young racehorses.'

'Isn't that why you hired them?'

He smiled in assent. 'Jonas is okay. Simon's got cold feet about his research.'

'He always was a wild card.'

'There's a lot riding on it.'

She took another sip of wine. 'You've betted on him to balance the books? I've heard the company's got financial problems.'

'Rumour travels fast.'

'Is it true?'

He shrugged. 'Enough for them to take risks that may be unwise.'

She observed him for a moment. 'And Simon's not what you'd call a team player.'

'So how should I handle him?'

'Listen to his woes, do what you can to appease them. He's an idealist, and the big stick won't do much good.'

'If I fail, he won't get his contract renewed. Someone

else with less scruples will finish the job, and I'll take the rap for hiring someone who wasn't up to it.'

Their food arrived and for a few minutes they turned their attention to it.

'You've cut your ties with the Firm?' Conrad said eventually.

She gave a surprised laugh. 'What's that supposed to mean?'

'Just curious.'

'Yes. I no longer believe in King and Country!'

'That never stopped you working for them.'

'I'm happy being an academic. You could say I've found the life that suits me. And you?'

He sat back in his chair. 'The same. I'm an R and D manager in a pharmaceutical company. That's enough of a challenge.'

She took a sip of her wine and nodded approval of his choice. 'So here's to Ireland!'

He raised his glass in response.

'Tell me about the rest of your life.'

'I don't really have one.'

'You're alone?'

'Yes. How about you?'

'Between lovers. One I've just sent packing, the other I haven't yet decided if it's worth pursuing or not.'

'Hard to please as ever!'

'No. Honest. I like sex but I don't want a relationship just for the sake of it.' She smiled. 'And you? Perhaps you're happy with casual encounters?'

'I'm not about to get entangled with someone just for the ride, as the Irish say.'

She laughed. 'Ah, with the Irish, everything comes down to horses!'

———

The streets of Dublin were quiet at three in the morning. Simon, Jonas and Fela were driving home in Simon's shiny second-hand four by four in a state of high exhilaration.

'I could have danced all night!' Fela sang dreamily from the back seat, where she was curled up under Simon's jacket.

'I told you those township guys would chase the blues away!' Jonas said. 'How's the car?'

'Amazing! 3 litres and only 50,000 on the clock.'

'I thought it was 20,000?'

'They made a mistake. So I got a week's trial for a small down-payment!'

'Remember that clapped out old Nissan we took to the Lakes!' Fela said. 'The radiator boiled three times and we got a puncture.'

'Two punctures! It rained all the way there and all the way back. And the windows wouldn't close... Okay, folks! Here's the motorway. Let's see what she's made of.'

He joined the fast-moving stream of traffic from the slip road, and weaving past the vehicle in front put his foot down. The car leapt forward.

———

Conrad, unable to sleep, made himself a nightcap, sat down on the sofa and turned on the TV. A lone figure, insignificant against the wind-blown canyons of Arizona, rode his horse into the sunset. His thoughts turned to Estelle. She was so confident in her increasing years, whereas he felt less and less sure about anything. He'd met her when they were both recruited into the Service. A brief affair had ripened into a friendship, one of the few he'd maintained over the years. Now she was educating young people towards a more fulfilling future, whereas he'd sold his soul to a pharmaceutical company whose only aim was profit.

There was no real surprise in that. Global capitalism had swallowed up the whole world, including, as Estelle agreed, academia. He'd known being stuck in an office day after day would be hard after the life he'd led. In his present mood even some failed mission into whatever foreign trouble-spot he and his men had been dropped, seemed more worthwhile than his present efforts. He was no more of a team player than Simon, which was why he respected him in spite of his youthful intransigence. Like everyone else, he'd pinned his hopes on the vaccine, believing it'd be a winner in the fight to help desperate children caught up in drought and post-colonial wars, a life-saver that would ensure the future of the company.

From the start he'd sensed Simon was a gamble, but one he'd believed worthwhile. And if he was right about the side effects, he should be listened to, whatever the cost. It needed another team to assess his claims, but the company's obsession with secrecy ruled that out. Every day Weiss was asking for a progress report, and now it seemed buyers were lined up to do business. His powerlessness infuriated him.

Involving Estelle was also risky. She owed no loyalty to the company, and was quite capable of sabotaging the deal if she believed it to be important, leaving him open to the accusation of leaking company secrets. When he'd taken this job, he'd believed himself done with the machinations of those shadowy figures who were once his masters. Their Machiavellian ways and die-hard Cold War attitudes that made them only too keen to pursue alliances with some of the most dangerous and repulsive people on the planet, were ultimately what drove him out. And now here he was, employing their methods.

It had begun so simply. As a youth, he'd gone abroad with the single intention of getting as far as possible from an abusive, unhappy home. After a drunken night in Marseille, he'd signed up with the Foreign Legion for seven years, and before he knew it he was being bullied and drilled into shape by a Sergeant Major, who left no room for doubt or reflection. Every waking moment was catered for, in a life designed to erase both individuality and all memory of a former existence. Two things only were required: discipline and obedience to one's superior officers. Sometimes, frustrated beyond endurance by the relentless fatigues and pettifogging rules about cleanliness and immaculate uniform, plus frustration at his incompetence with the French language, he determined to abscond. But the fear of being caught, and the punishment that awaited, stopped him. Besides, where would he go?

Gradually his French improved, and he found himself

in Corsica as part of the Second Foreign Parachute Regiment, stationed in Calvi. The exhilaration of leaping out of an aircraft into pure blue air, and the frisson of fear before the parachute opened to slow his fall, quickly became an addiction. Bit by bit, the bunch of misfits who were his fellow soldiers became the family he'd never known, and in one of the commanding officers, noted for his concern for the well-being of his young recruits, he found the authority figure he'd always sought. Whatever murderous conflicts they were dropped into, as a highly trained, tight-knit unit their purpose was clear and their unquestioning mutual reliance the closest he'd come to love.

After the seven years of his contract were over, he returned to England with no contacts or emotional ties, desperately missing the fellowship of his former comrades. The only life he knew was with the military, so he joined the British army with the intention of getting an education. Studying for a degree meant his military duties mainly involved the training of recruits. But army life in England was entirely different from the Legion. Though on the surface more relaxed, class divisions, especially with Sandhurst trained officers, were far more rigid. There he'd been part of a hierarchy that included both officers and men, united in a bond that overrode class or nationality. Here, though nominally an officer, he was a fish out of water, a perception he knew his colleagues shared.

Having attained his master's degree in the management of human resources, he left the army and was approached by the secret services to run a mission on the basis of contacts he'd made in one of the world's worst trouble spots. At first he was happy to be contributing to the safety and well-being of the nation, but it didn't take him long to become disillusioned. Nothing was as it seemed, and the double-dealing disgusted him. Armed with a Ph.D, he'd accepted the job with Associated Swiss Pharmaceuticals, partly because it meant living in Ireland, a country with no connection to the British establishment or its long history of global exploitation.

And now he was once more aligned on the side of people whose capacity for unscrupulous greed was at least equal to his previous masters', albeit for money rather than power and influence. In the end, he suspected, that boiled down to much the same thing. When governments and centres of learning lost their independence to the pressures of global capitalism, few alternatives remained. Sometimes he thought of going off to some wild desert place and hiring himself out to the first bidder, but that was merely a pipe dream.

Estelle had asked if he was lonely, and he'd answered sincerely that he wasn't, perhaps the fruit of years of peripatetic living where relationships were fleeting. Some of the men in the Parachute Regiment had taken up with local Calvi girls, and established families they rarely saw and seemed to take little interest in. He'd observed them at local dances or village fetes, joking and drinking with their mates while the young women sat isolated and ignored. He'd felt pity for those neglected pretty girls, each with a child on her knee, all of them strangers to the man who wanted nothing more than to be back with his comrades. He'd determined never to commit the same folly. What was the point, if love was so transitory?

Just once he believed he'd found something lasting.

The woman was half Ghanaian, half Norwegian, a photo-journalist, and for several years they'd run into one another in different parts of Africa, snatching whatever time they could to be together. He remembered the excitement he'd felt before each encounter. He'd even begun to dream of a possible future together, in England or perhaps Norway. Then she was sent to the Far East, and it became harder and harder to meet up. Eventually he'd learned she was having an affair with an Egyptian war correspondent, and what hurt him most was that she didn't tell him. They'd always sworn to say when it was over, and it devastated him to think she no longer cared enough to go through the painful task of informing him there was another man in her life. A year later he received a letter, which he tore up and threw away unread.

Since then he'd had affairs, most too casual to remember. And now he found himself observing his young assistant, and the way her unruly black hair fell into two soft wings as she bent her head over her keyboard, exposing a silky triangle of pale brown skin. Perhaps she reminded him of that other woman, and he did his best not to give it much thought. But in the morning, usually after he'd already been at work for an hour or more, when he heard the door to her office open and close and quick footsteps cross the floor of the neighbouring room, he felt an unfamiliar lifting of his heart. He did his best to ignore it. She was years younger than him and he had no desire to complicate his existence. But feelings weren't so easily regulated.

———

Fela took off her coat, hung it on a peg behind the door and went to her desk. She leafed through the post, put to one side what she considered important, and dumped the rest in her in tray. She opened up her computer and began to go through her emails. One sent from Head Office in Geneva caught her attention. It included the minutes of a recent meeting about the allocation of funds for R and D. She printed it out and knocked on Conrad's door.

'Come in!'

She entered and placed the email in front of him. 'I thought you ought to take a look at this. And Dr Weiss wants a meeting to update him on our progress.'

He noticed the dark rings under her eyes. It was barely a month since her father died, but he sensed this wasn't the moment for compassion.

'Leave it to me. I'll talk to him.'

She turned to go.

'There's something I want to ask you.'

She hesitated.

'You've known Simon a long time?'

'Yes.'

'Would you call him impulsive?'

She considered a moment. 'He's moody, a bit rash sometimes... Why are you asking?'

'He's frustrated and it's affecting his work. I need to know if he's planning something he might regret.'

'And you want me to spy on him?' Anger brought a flush to her cheeks. 'Perhaps you'd better ask him yourself.'

'I just want to keep him out of trouble.'

'I'm afraid I'm not the person to ask,' she said, and turned back to her room.

'Well done!' Conrad muttered to himself.

She sat down at her desk, stiff with anger. Simon was her friend and she wasn't about to inform on him behind his back. Yet it was true he'd been behaving oddly of late, and at times he and Jonas seemed more rivals than friends. Once she'd been in love with Simon, but he was becoming increasingly unreachable. Since her father died, she found herself turning to Jonas.

Whenever she thought of her father, it was as if the air were being sucked out of her, just as all his music and laughter had been sucked down into the grave.

By lunchtime, after a morning trying to itemise R and D's expenditures over the previous year in preparation for Conrad's meeting with Weiss, her eyes were sore and her head throbbed. She decided to take a break for lunch.

The muzak in the lift jangled rather than soothed her, so she took the stairs and walked quickly through the foyer, past the security guard and onto the street. Outside the air was fresher, though tainted with the smell of diesel, and the sun emerged from behind a bank of clouds.

At the row of shops known as the village, she bought a miso soup and a box of salad from the Japanese take-away, and carried them to a bench in the nearby park popular with the lunchtime office crowd. The soup needed a few minutes to cool. She stared down at the leaves of spinach and curly endive embellished with noodles and pale pieces of tofu, and realised she'd lost her appetite. Even when her mother died after two excruciating months suffering from an undiagnosed ovarian cancer, she'd scarcely felt this low. Grief had been tempered by relief at knowing her mother was out of her misery at last. Now all she wanted was to curl up and hibernate. But winter was over, and the air was filled with the chatter of people enjoying the spring sunshine.

She looked up and saw Conrad approaching.

'D'you mind if I sit down?'

She nodded, though in no mood for conversation. For a while neither of them spoke, as she took sips from her polystyrene cup.

'I'm sorry I offended you earlier. I was out of order,' he said eventually.

'Yes.'

'Anyway, I've a suggestion.'

She glanced at him warily.

'Take the rest of the afternoon off and give me a lift on your bike to my place. I can play you some recordings of your father's music.'

'Maybe I could just borrow them?'

'The best are vinyl. You probably haven't got a suitable player.'

She hesitated. Hearing Sean play would stir up memories she wasn't sure she was ready for.

'My offer is partly selfish. I've also a passion for bikes.

You could give me a ride to my place, and I'd lend you the CDs.'

The unspoken camaraderie of bikers softened her resistance. In any case she had no desire to return to the office.

'Okay.' She stood up, leaving her uneaten lunch on the bench for whatever homeless drifter might come foraging after dark.

In the company car park, she fumbled in her bag for the keys to her bike and offered them to Conrad.

'You can drive, if you want.'

'Really? I didn't like to ask!'

She handed him a helmet and took the pillion seat.

'I once had a Harley,' he said over his shoulder. 'My pride and joy!'

'My father's got a Norton.' She couldn't bring herself to use the past tense.

'Both great bikes! 100mph down the motorway and no vibrations. Like riding the wind!'

He revved up the engine and they set off. It was some time since she'd been a passenger. The tar-like smell of his waxed jacket reminded her with a pang of Sean, and she did her best to synchronise her body to the bike's movements without holding on too tightly. A couple of miles south of Dún Laoghaire they turned off the motorway, and at length pulled up at a small harbour beside a row of three fishermen's cottages.

'This is it.'

He cut the engine and waited for her to dismount. The air smelled fresh and mildly fishy. Moored to the quay were two or three boats and from the empty creels and bits of equipment strewn about the quayside the place was clearly still a working harbour.

'It'll be okay to leave the bike here,' he said, handing her the key and his helmet.

Inside the cottage, the living room opened out from a narrow hallway, with a window that ran almost the length of one wall and a magnificent view of the sea. For a moment she was almost blinded by the brightness that flooded in off the water, throwing patterns of light and shade onto the ceiling. A large abstract painting took up most of one wall and on the adjacent one a row of book-shelves ran the height of the room, with small African sculptures in wood or moulded clay in the spaces between volumes. The room had a quiet, uncluttered air, like a library except for the brightness of the light. It was not at all what she expected of the man of action she assumed Conrad to be.

She went over to the bookshelves and glanced at the titles. There were books about travel and wildlife, novels and poetry, and several volumes about the collapse of the Soviet Union and the subsequent rise of the mafias. Open on the low table was a large book on African art.

'Make yourself at home. Would you like something to drink, or eat? I noticed you didn't eat your lunch.'

'Maybe a coffee.'

While he was in the kitchen, she picked out a book about the conflict in Somalia, written in French.

'You read French?' she asked as he returned.

'Yes.'

He placed a tray with cups, milk and sugar on the low table. 'Have you spent time in France?'

'Several years.'

'How come?'

'I was based there.' He paused. 'In the Legion you speak only French.'

'The Foreign Legion?' She couldn't disguise her surprise.

'My father once took me to see a film, *Beau Geste*, I think it was. I must have been about ten. It was about a legionnaire. Very brave and dashing!'

He smiled as he handed her the coffee he'd just poured. 'And not very realistic! Help yourself to milk and sugar.'

She sipped her coffee as he went over to a cabinet and selected a couple of the vinyl records stacked there, which he placed on the table next to the book on African art.

'These are Sean's. Choose something and I'll play it.'

'You choose. You obviously know his stuff far better than me.'

He picked out a disc and handed her the sleeve. 'This one's recorded live. It's one of my favourites.' He placed the disc on the turntable.

Far from distressing, the music brought back all the joy of Sean's playing. When the track finished and Conrad lifted the arm on the record player, she cried out in protest.

'Let it run! They played that number at my first live gig.'

She closed her eyes, losing herself in the music. When she opened them, Conrad was no longer there and she could hear someone moving around in the kitchen. Unable to remain still, she stood up and began to dance, twisting and turning through patterns of light and shade as the fiddle called to her.

She came to with the sound of clapping as the track finished. A young man stood in the doorway observing her. He was barefoot and wore a long white robe.

'Bravo!'

She stood still, mortified at being caught unawares. His footsteps made no sound, and as he moved through the room a fine white dust rose from his clothes. His skin was almost blue-black and his striking features reminded her of one of Conrad's African masks. He disappeared into the kitchen and she heard remarks being exchanged and a brief burst of laughter.

She was hunting for her jacket when Conrad came back into the room, followed by the young man.

'Fela, this is Tomas,' he said. 'He's here for a couple of weeks preparing for an exhibition of his sculptures in town. You should come. I promise you it'll be worth it.'

Tomas came towards her and held out his hand. His skin felt rough to the touch.

'Excuse the dust!' he said, pulling in his robe. 'I'm working on a plaster maquette. It gets everywhere.' His accent sounded French.

'Tomas is from Mali,' said Conrad.

'Don't let me interrupt your dancing!' said Tomas, making no effort to hide his amusement.

'It's not something I usually do before an audience,' she retorted frostily. 'I'd best be off.'

'If it's on my account, I'm leaving for the gallery as soon as I've changed.'

'It's not. I've things to do.' She looked around for her jacket.

'Let me at least give you some CDs,' said Conrad.

He selected three and handed them to her. 'If you like them, keep them.'

R iding home, she thought about the humiliation Tomas had made her feel. Conrad at home might be different from the man she encountered each day at work, but it was the sudden appearance of Tomas that had thrown her. She'd met with that mocking response from certain black activists she'd encountered in London, their air of ironic disapproval as though they saw through the dishonesty of her disguise – a brown woman imperson-ating those who were white and privileged, a 'coconut'. To her father's people, even though they welcomed her as a stranger, she was black. She existed in a kind of limbo, impossible to identify with either side.

L ater that afternoon Conrad returned to his office. Checking his recent emails, he found one from Simon.

'This is my statement for you to relay at the board meeting with Weiss, as it seems I'm not invited to speak for myself.'

Attached was a single page containing a short descrip-tion of the risks of internal bleeding, severe attacks of diarrhoea, and respiratory problems that could be brought on, especially in children, if the vaccine was administered in its present form. He spelt out the additional problem that since children in the developing world have greater exposure to disease than in first world countries, trials of the drug's effectiveness and different levels of dosage needed in different regions must also be carried out before a vaccine could be licensed. He offered no timetable for how long it would take to carry out such tests, nor any further scientific evidence. In addition there was a note addressed to Conrad. 'Such trials are no doubt what they plan to carry out in some under-developed country, prior to marketing the product in the far more lucrative markets of the developed world. Once again poor people are being experimented on!'

Conrad deleted the personal note then printed out the attachment.

———

Jonas was at work in his lab, when the door opened and Conrad entered without knocking.

'I'm looking for Simon. You wouldn't happen to know where he is?'

'Not in his lab?'

'No. I need to see him urgently, before the meeting with the Board tomorrow.'

'If I hear from him, I'll tell him to contact you.'

'Please do!'

'Have you seen this?' Jonas's assistant said, as soon as Conrad had left the room.

Jonas went over to his computer screen, which showed CCTV images of a technician in protective clothing entering a hangar and throwing a switch. At once fine needles of water rained down onto the plants below, creating a whitish mist. From another camera, a child walked between two rows of plants with a watering can. A man appeared, grabbed the child and hurried her away. Jonas ran the footage back, and freezing on the man's face recognised Sean O'Connor.

'Who sent this?'

'Their security manager. He thought it worth reporting.'

He released the footage and fast-forwarded it to the end.

'Tell them they need to step up security and delete it.'

———

Simon turned out of the company forecourt and headed off along the road that led away from the village. He had little idea where he was going, nor any concern for the cars that thundered past him when the pavement petered out. His frustration had been boiling for days, making it impossible to think clearly. He'd known the job would entail compromises, but not how disgusted the whole thing would make him feel. Against all his principles he'd joined the ranks of those whose sole priority was to make money, and it was nobody's fault but his own. Dr Murphy, his predecessor, had identified harmful side effects in the original vaccine, which so far he'd been unable to remedy. Going ahead with it in its present form would mean experimenting on some of the world's poorest and most desperate people already weakened by hunger and disease. And even if trials were ultimately successful, they'd most likely be priced out of receiving the benefits. Weiss refused to listen or let him put his case in Geneva. He was left with one option, but that was so radical he must be sure and as yet he hadn't made up his mind.

———

It was after six, and most of the workforce had gone home. In Simon's lab, a man wearing a white lab coat and the face mask used for working on experiments, locked the door from the inside and went over to Simon's desk. He switched on his computer and pulled a notebook out of his pocket in which various passwords were written. He sat down and typed in '3musketeers'. It was refused. He consulted the notebook and tried again with 'dartagnan1forall', followed by a six digit mathematical formula. The computer opened up. He connected an extra hard drive to the machine, and set to work making copies of the files.

———

When Fela reached home it was almost dark. The clocks were due to go forward at the weekend then the evenings would get lighter. She parked her bike outside her house and walked to the sea. The remains of the sunset lent a metallic sheen to the water, and seagulls wheeled and screeched above a fishing boat returning to harbour. The scent of diesel mingled with the smell of fish made her faintly nauseous, and she struggled to throw off her gloom. She knew her irritability and moodiness had tried the patience of Simon and Jonas. It was time to break out from the mouse wheel of her thoughts and put things right.

She took her mobile from her pocket and dialled Simon's number. It went straight to answerphone so she dialled Jonas. He answered after a couple of rings.

'Hi, Fela! How's it going?'

'Are you still in your lab?'

'I'm just leaving. D'you have a suggestion?'

'We could go for a drink. Or I could come over to your place?'

'I'll be home in half an hour. Just need to pick up a couple of things from the store. Why don't you come round.'

'Great! I'll come and amuse you while you cook!'

Feeling better, she replaced the phone in her pocket.

An hour later she rang Jonas's doorbell, and was buzzed into the building. Good smells leaked into the corridor from the open door of his flat. He was in the kitchen, putting a casserole into the oven.

'Drink? Food'll be another half hour.'

'I brought this.'

She placed a bottle of Burgundy on the table.

'Great. Glasses are over there.' He gestured towards the cupboard.

'You're turning into a culinary genius! Less than an hour ago you were in the office, and now this!'

'I prepared it yesterday. Otherwise I'm too hungry to wait and start snacking.'

'I admire you. I'm not much of a cook.'

'So at least I'm better at something.'

He took some cutlery out of a drawer and began to set the table.

She took a sip of her wine. 'Is Simon coming?'

'Who knows?'

'I've called and texted him. Radio silence! D'you think he's gone to see that ex-tutor of his, Estelle?'

'Maybe.'

'I think they might be having an affair.'

Jonas let out a burst of laughter.

'I'm serious! Did you see how he reacted when he spotted her at your prize giving?'

'I think she prefers older men.'

'He's just so secretive these days. If he's bothered about his work, she might be the person he'd go to for advice.'

'Ask him. He rarely confides in me.' He finished laying the table and began preparing a salad.

'So you don't know what's bugging him?'

'No more than you. The company have a client lined up to buy his vaccine. He's insisting on more time, which Weiss is refusing to give.'

The doorbell went. Jonas picked up the intercom. 'It's Simon. Lost his key!' he said, as he buzzed him in.

A few moments later Simon entered, looking dishevelled. 'Any chance of a drink?'

Jonas took another glass from the cupboard and poured some wine. It was clear it wasn't Simon's first.

'Why haven't you been answering your phone?' Fela demanded.

'I left it in the lab.'

'I don't believe you!'

'Let's go out dancing!' Simon said, ignoring her remark.

'Supper's ready. Why don't we eat first?'

'Who needs food?'

'Me, for one. Jonas has been cooking.'

'I came back because I got your texts.'

'Well, hang on while we eat.'

He sat down and took a swig of his wine. Jonas laid out another plate, knife and fork.

'It's the weekend. I need fun not food! Let's hit town!'

'Not with you driving!'

'So no takers?'

'Yes. But what's the hurry?' Jonas said soothingly.

'I don't have time for this. See you both later.' He stood up.

'Where are you going?'

'Wherever the wind takes me,' he said with an airy wave of his hand.

'Don't be an arsehole!' Jonas retorted.

But Simon had already disappeared through the door.

'We should go after him. He's going to do something stupid.'

'He's not that far gone. Let's eat first,' said Jonas.

―――――――

S imon took off in the direction of the city. But after a mile or so he changed his mind, did a U turn, and pulled up in the car park of the company building. Driving had sobered him up, though the amount he'd drunk loosened his inhibitions. It was after nine, and only the security lights in the corridors and main foyer were lit. The night guard was seated at the desk reading the evening paper. Simon showed his pass, wished him good evening, and made his way to the lift. When he reached his floor he unlocked his lab and locked it again behind him. He took his mobile out of his pocket and dialled a number.

'Estelle? It's me, Simon. I need to see you. Yes, now. Could you come to my lab?… Thanks. Call when you get here. I'll come down and let you in.'

Fifteen minutes went by, twenty. He paced up and down. What was taking Estelle so long? He picked up his phone and dialled again. After several rings it went to answerphone. He flung it down on the desk in frustration. A moment later it went. He grabbed it.

'Simon, I'm so sorry,' Estelle's voice came through. 'Something's come up. I'll call you later. Soon as I can.'

'Forget it!' he snapped, switched off his phone and shoved it in his pocket.

Coldly sober now, he went over to his computer and began to dismantle the hard drive. He grabbed the wheeled shopping bag his assistant, Paul, always kept near the coat hooks by the door, went over to the fridge where the vaccine samples were stored, unlocked it and emptied the contents into the shopping bag. Next he went over to his desk and shoved the hard drive, its backup, and several bulky paper files in with the samples. Dragging the shopping bag behind him, he unlocked the door of his lab and peered into the corridor. It was silent and empty. Everyone had gone home for the weekend. Apart from the night porter in the foyer and a security guard doing his rounds, the only person in the building would be Maloney, the chief caretaker, holed up in the control room near the main staircase. With luck he'd be too absorbed in some football game or brewing up to keep much of an eye on the CCTV monitors.

He decided to take the stairs in case the sound of the lift alerted attention. His trainers made no noise on the concrete steps, though the wheels of the trolley squeaked whenever its weight forced him to put it to the ground. He reached the basement and turned left along the corridor that led to the boiler room where the furnace was. He'd been down here a couple of times to dispose of small quantities of waste insufficiently toxic to be included in the official collection. He paused for a moment in front of the heavy fireproof swing doors. He didn't switch on the light in case they'd recently installed a CCTV camera, though the only one he'd noticed so far was at the end of the corridor covering the exit door.

He pushed open the fire doors and was greeted by the subdued roar of the furnace. Even from this distance he could feel the force of its dragon breath. He took down a protective mask from a hook on the wall, a leather apron and pair of thick, gauntleted gloves from a nearby shelf. A couple of wheeled metal carts designed as shovels were lined up against one wall. He selected one, tipped out the contents of his shopping bag, put on the gloves, apron and mask and approached the furnace. He pressed the green button that operated the door. It moved aside, emitting a blast of intolerable heat. Instinctively he stepped back. Then, grasping the handles of the cart, he tipped its cargo into the flames.

He stood there for a moment longer, staring into the red maw, then pressed the button to enclose its terrifying force and moved back. If anything survived it would only be traces of the hard drives' metal casing, and those could never be identified. He took off his gloves and helmet, wiped his sleeve across his damp brow and ran his fingers over his prickling scalp. He returned the gloves and apron to the shelf, hung up the helmet, stowed away the cart and walked back down the passage to the staircase, pulling the shopping bag after him. With a bit of luck, no one would ever know he'd been there.

When he reached the foyer, the night porter wasn't at his desk. Most likely he was in the toilet or chatting to Maloney. He decided not to bother returning the shopping bag to his lab and exited the building, using his pass. In the car park he put the bag into the boot and got into his shiny new car. He felt no sense of triumph at having taken matters into his own hands, only a profound exhaustion. He laid his head against the steering wheel and fell asleep.

Twenty minutes later he woke with a start, uncertain how long he'd been out. He started the engine. His only thought was to get away from the city, and when he reached the crossroads he turned south. The road was deserted except for the headlights of a distant car in his rear view mirror. He put his foot down and at the next exit left the motorway and sped off in the direction of the

Wicklow Mountains. He had no plan, and it would be Monday before anyone would think of looking for him. By that time he would have figured out what to do next. Destroying his research was a crime, for which he could probably go to prison. It was certainly the end of his career as a scientist. He shivered. Night was coming on and the temperature was dropping. He reached into the glove box for the hip flask he kept there and took a swig.

Small roads wound up into faintly looming hills. He met no other cars, and apart from a vague outline of distant horizon he could see nothing of the landscape. He tried not to think about the irrevocable nature of what he'd done. His one regret was that the months, probably years, of work he'd destroyed were not merely his own but also his unknown predecessor, Murphy's. He wondered if Murphy would hear of what had happened and how he would feel. If only Estelle had answered his call. He'd intended to lodge a copy of the formula with her for safe-keeping, a bargaining counter to use in his battle with the company. Instead in his anger and frustration he'd destroyed everything, and even if he escaped the law he'd never be employed again. He was too tired to think any more. All he could do was to keep driving until sleep forced him to pull over.

He took another swig from the hip flask, then reached into the side pocket of the car door for a CD and shoved it into the slot on the dashboard. Bruce Springsteen rang out into the darkness and outside a fine drizzle had begun to fall. He turned on the wipers, blinking as headlights from an approaching car dazzled him in the rear view mirror then disappeared with the curve of the road. As the road straightened they were back again, almost blinding him. He flashed his headlights to indicate to the driver to lower his, and when they didn't was forced to twist his mirror away. A blast from the car's horn made him start. He gripped the steering wheel and glanced in the side mirror. The car was now so close it was almost touching his bumper and there was no room for it to pass. The guy must be crazy!

Enraged, he swung out into the centre of the road and put his foot down. He wasn't about to be shoved into the ditch. As soon as the road widened he'd pull over and let the idiot pass. The speeding hedgerows gave way to stone walls and open moorland as the two cars gathered pace. Suddenly he felt a massive blow from behind. The steering wheel shook in his hands, and his vehicle bounced over a rough patch in the road. The lights of the other filled his car and his head lurched back against the rest as he swerved towards the ditch. Another blow from behind propelled his car into a spin. 'Fuck you, you bastard!' he yelled, just as his side of the car hit the ground and his door burst open, catapulting him onto the ground and a waiting rock.

A few feet away his car hung suspended in mid-air against the wall, wheels spinning, engine hissing, as if at any moment it would burst into flames. The other car had halted a few metres behind, but no one emerged as if awaiting an imminent explosion.

———

On Saturday morning Fela woke late after a poor night's sleep. She made herself a coffee and returned to bed with her laptop. Top of her list of emails was one from Simon, sent the previous evening. It said he was taking off for the weekend and wouldn't be in touch till Monday. It wasn't the first time he'd gone AWOL when upset or angry, only to return a day or two later sober and ready to make amends.

Her phone went. It was Conrad. He didn't usually call her over the weekend and she felt a rush of anxiety.

'Are you busy?'

'Not specially. Why?'

'It's been a tough week and I was thinking I might invite you to lunch.'

'Any particular reason?' she said lightly.

'I made lasagne last night. If you fancy that with a salad you'd be very welcome.'

'What about Tomas?'

'He's at the gallery.'

She paused for a moment.

'Yes, lasagne sounds good. What time?'

'One-ish?'

'Okay. I'll be there.'

At one fifteen she parked her bike outside his cottage and rang the bell. He opened the door, welcomed her in and took her jacket, which he hung on a nearby peg. He was wearing a pair of well-worn cord trousers and a fisherman's sweater instead of his usual office clothes, which suited him she thought.

'Make yourself at home. I'll bring some drinks. Lunch will be a few minutes.'

In the living room she was struck again by the kaleido-scopic brilliance of the light. Being here, just the two of them on a purely social visit, felt a little strange. They weren't exactly friends. She wasn't quite sure what they were, but it was pleasant.

He brought her a glass of wine and invited her into the kitchen, where the table was laid for lunch. The lasagne smelt delicious and she realised how hungry she was.

'You're quite a cook!' she said, after a couple of mouthfuls.

'I do a few things well, but it's not exactly a wide repertoire.'

She turned her attention to the food and for a few moments they ate in silence.

'If something's troubling you, apart from your father's death you must tell me,' Conrad said at length.

'Nothing in particular.'

She didn't want to spoil the atmosphere with heavy talk. But Conrad wasn't letting go. 'I wondered if you were worried about Simon?'

'Well, yes. But I guess whatever's wrong he'll get over it. He usually does.'

'This time I think it's more serious. He has a crisis of conscience that won't be easy to resolve.'

'He's talked to you?'

'Not much. And you?'

She shook her head. 'He's talked about the vaccine not being ready. But what exactly he intends to do about it, I've no idea.'

Conrad's phone rang in another room. He excused himself and went into the hall, where he'd left it in his coat pocket.

She strained to hear what he was saying, but his voice was too quiet. Eventually she heard him thank someone and ring off. It was a couple of minutes before he returned to the kitchen. When he did so, his grim expression warned her of calamity. He came and stood behind her chair, resting his hands on her shoulders. The tension of waiting for him to speak was almost unbearable.

'There's bad news. It's Simon. He's had an accident.'

She twisted round to face him. 'How bad?'

'The worst.' He paused. 'He's dead.'

She let out a cry like a wounded animal and leapt to her feet, making to flee. He caught her and held her tightly against him, feeling the heart pounding in her chest as sobs choked her.

W hen she opened her eyes it was bright day and sun filtered into the room through the slits of half-closed Venetian blinds. She had no idea what time it was or where she was. She turned her head to gaze at the unfamiliar room, as bit by bit consciousness returned. She was at Conrad's and something terrible had happened, something she could scarcely bear to think about.

The door opened and Conrad came into the room, carrying a mug of coffee and a slice of toast and honey on a tray. He set it down on the bedside table and sat down beside the bed. She pulled herself upright and moved the duvet slightly aside. She was still dressed.

'What time is it?'

'Seven thirty. I gave you a mild sedative. It seemed best. At least you slept.'

'For how long?'

'Over twelve hours.'

Memory returned like a hand on the throat. Simon was dead.

'Drink your coffee.' He reached for her hand that was resting on the duvet.

'Where is he? I want to see him.'

'We're waiting to hear from the police in Wicklow. As soon as we know more, I'll drive you.'

'Does Jonas know?'

'I spoke to him a few minutes ago. He's coming over.'

She withdrew her hand and covered her face.

———

Conrad arrived at the company offices, having left Jonas with Fela at his house. Since it was Sunday, he met no one except the security guards at the entrance. As he unlocked the door to Simon's lab, he was met by a strange, stale smell. He paused for a moment then walked over to the far wall where a row of four cages stood on a wide metal shelf. Inside a dozen white mice lay rigid in death, mouths open as though gasping for breath, small pink paws stretched out in a pathetic plea for help.

As he stood gazing, the door opened and Paul, Simon's assistant, entered.

'What are you doing here?' he said, stopping short.

'More important, what's the hell's happened here?' Conrad gestured towards the cages.

Paul came closer to take a look. 'Jesus!'

Conrad turned to him. 'What brings you in on a Sunday?'

'I was off sick on Friday. I came by to see how Simon had left things before the meeting on Monday.'

Without further explanation, Paul went over to Simon's computer and pressed the keys. The screen remained blank. He moved on to his own computer and did the same, again without response.

'The hard drives have been removed!'

'Christ! Did you know he was going to do something like this?' Conrad was barely able to contain his rage.

'Of course not! I just knew he was worried.' Paul went over to the fridge where the samples were kept. It was empty. He opened the metal cupboard where files and other sensitive material were locked up for safety at weekends and opened it.

'Even the back ups have gone!'

He shut the cupboard door then moved aside quickly, as though fearful Conrad might be about to hit him. But Conrad remained still, doing his best to master his fury.

'If you suspected something like this, why the hell didn't you tell me? You worked with him, for God's sake! You surely realised he was on the verge of doing something drastic?'

Paul mumbled something and shook his head.

Conrad went over to the window that looked out over the car park, empty now because it was Sunday, and for a moment neither of them spoke.

Eventually he turned back to Paul.

'Make sure you say nothing to anyone. Go home and leave this to me.'

He waited for Paul to leave, then locked the lab and took the stairs to the floor above and his office. He was trying to think what to do next. Obviously Weiss must be told, and also about Simon's death. If the police hadn't already informed him, Conrad wanted to be the first to break the news. And it needed to be done before Monday.

He sat down at his desk and dialled the personal number Weiss had given him for emergencies. Eventually the phone was picked up and a strange male voice answered.

'Hello, can I speak to Dr Weiss, please.'

'Who is this?'

'Conrad Dreyer.'

There was a pause.

Then the man said, 'Just a minute.'

He heard voices in the background and eventually Weiss came on the line. 'Conrad! I hope this is important. It's Sunday.'

'I'm afraid it is, sir.'

'Oh Lord! Don't tell me we've got more problems with your young protégé?'

Conrad paused. 'I've just been in his lab. It seems he's removed the hard drives from the computers and also made off with the samples.'

'I knew that young idiot was trouble when you hired him!'

He was angry, but more restrained than Conrad had

expected. 'You said you could handle him, and now look what he's done!'

'I'm afraid that's not all.'

'There's more?'

'Simon was killed in the early hours of yesterday in a car accident.'

There was a brief moment of silence.

'So how come you're telling me this shocking news today? I should have been informed straight away!'

'The police only confirmed it last night. I decided to wait till morning to call you.'

It was stretching the truth a little but that scarcely mattered.

'This is an appalling disaster. What do you suggest we do now?'

'I'll drive down to Wicklow, see if I can get a few more details. It's possible he had the hard drives with him.'

'Good idea. Call me as soon as you get there. And keep this to yourself. We don't want it getting about till we know exactly where we are. God, I knew he was trouble, but nothing like this!'

Conrad switched off his phone. He wondered whether or not to tell Fela about driving to Wicklow. She would most likely insist on coming with him, and that wouldn't help either of them. The police had made it clear they weren't ready to release Simon's body. But he might get a look at his car and, if it had already been searched, find out what the police had found.

He locked his office and went down to the car park where he'd left his Jeep. Before he drove off, he decided to call Estelle. If Simon had confided in anyone it would be her. The call went to answerphone and he left a brief message, asking her to call him back as soon as possible.

He took the coast road and picked up the motorway at Bray. The traffic was heavy, but it gave him time to think. He went over what the Garda had told him. The accident had happened shortly after midnight, and they didn't yet know whether anyone else was involved. They'd said nothing about finding anything in the car, but perhaps they hadn't fully searched it yet. If the hard drives went missing, it might well spell disaster for the company in the current financial crisis – relocation to Switzerland with a catastrophic loss of jobs. Weiss had already threatened as much, and it was impossible to know whether or not the threat was idle.

He reached Wicklow in the early afternoon and went straight to the Garda Station. After identifying himself to the desk sergeant, he was directed to a small room, where he was greeted by one of the senior detectives. The detective was friendly but not forthcoming. The accident, he insisted, was still under investigation, which would resume on Monday. All he could say was that it appeared Simon had lost control of his vehicle, probably by falling asleep at the wheel. A passing driver had found his car overturned in the ditch and called an ambulance, but by the time it reached hospital he was already dead.

'Where's the car now?' Conrad asked.

'In police custody, awaiting examination by forensics.'

'Could I take a look at it?'

'I'm afraid not, sir. As soon as we've finished our investigations, we'll let you know.'

'Do you have Dr. Eastlake's personal belongings? It's very important nothing goes missing.'

'Of course. They'll be returned as soon as we're through.'

He stood up. There seemed little point in further discussion.

On his way out he stopped by the desk sergeant, who was idly flicking through a cycling magazine, and asked if he could direct him to the car pound as he'd left some important documents in his car. Something about his authoritative manner must have impressed the bored sergeant, because he told him to go to the back of the building and turn left.

The gate to the pound was manned by a youth in a small hut, playing a game on his iPad, and as it was Sunday no one else was around. The youth barely glanced up when Conrad announced he needed to fetch something from his car, but nodded and returned to his game. Several rows of vehicles in various stages of damage were parked up in numbered bays. He walked along until he came to a black four-wheel drive he thought he recognised.

The damage seemed to be mainly on one side, running from the rear to the driver's front wing. Otherwise the car was newer and shinier than most. He tried the doors. They were locked. He pressed his face against one of the windows. The interior was completely bare as if thoroughly cleaned out. He tried the boot but that too was either jammed or locked. He walked around the car, photographing it from different angles on his phone. Especially he noted a big dent on the rear driver's side and a cracked number plate. The detective had said nothing about the car being struck from behind, though that was what it looked like, a hefty blow that would have sent it into a spin. Then, before anyone got curious, he made his way back to the entrance.

———

I t was after nine when he entered O'Shea's in the centre of Dublin. He'd managed to reach Estelle just before he set off for home and arranged to meet her there. She was seated in a booth at the back of the bar, reading a book. She looked up as he approached and smiled a greeting.

'I got you your usual.'

A double shot of Jameson's with water on the side, stood waiting on the table.

'Thanks.'

He sat down, glancing at the book she was reading – *Biopiracy* by someone called Vandana Shiva. Estelle pushed the menu towards him.

'I guess you could do with something to eat.'

'Indeed!'

She motioned for the waiter.

They ordered a goat cheese salad for her and lamb chops for him. He took a sip of his whisky, relishing the burning sensation in his throat.

'This is awful news!' Estelle said. 'Simon was so promising. All his bright future gone!'

'When did you find out?'

'Jonas called me this morning. He's devastated. We all are.'

Conrad felt her eyes on him as he took another drink.

'Do you think it was an accident?'

'Why d'you say that?' He kept his tone neutral.

'A lot was riding on that young man. What about his research?'

'What about it?'

'He was threatening to destroy it.'

Conrad hesitated. 'His lab's been cleaned out.'

For a moment she was silent in disbelief. 'Have you told anyone else?'

'No. I was waiting to speak to you. And it's important to keep it to yourself for the time being.'

Estelle fell silent.

'Someone may have followed him, thinking he had it with him,' Conrad said.

'Is there any evidence?'

He opened his phone and showed her the pictures he'd taken at the pound.

'Those marks make it look as if it was rammed from behind. The police are treating it as an accident.'

'But you think it was deliberate?'

'It's highly possible.'

'And the police found nothing in the car?'

'So far they won't say. Though with something that important they'd surely inform the company.'

'Maybe Simon hid the stuff before he left?'

'So why drive to the mountains?'

'Perhaps he just wanted time to cool off. I'm surprised they let you see the car.'

'They didn't know. I went to the pound.'

She smiled and nodded.

'I need your help, Estelle.'

'How?'

'If someone has got hold of those hard drives, something might surface. I believe the Agency keeps an eye on international markets.'

'Arms, maybe, not ordinary commerce.'

'You might stir their interest.'

'What makes you think I've still got contacts?'

'You have contacts in the scientific community. That's a start.'

'It's not like the old days, Conrad… Still, for Simon's sake I'll do what I can.'

'Thanks.'

She emptied her glass and signalled to the waiter to bring another. 'I like what I do. I like teaching and students. You, on the other hand, were always too much of a loner to make a good company man. So what are your reasons for doing what you do?'

'Earning a living. Having enough money to live in peace and do the things I enjoy.'

'Settling down at last!'

'If so, I'm not making a very good job of it.'

She gave a short laugh.

The waiter arrived with their food and another glass of wine for Estelle.

'The scientific community's a small world, riddled with spies of the industrial sort. If someone else has got hold of Simon's hard drives, you'd be likely to hear about it,' Conrad said, when the waiter had left.

'You credit me with insider knowledge I'm afraid I don't possess.'

He looked exhausted and she felt a sudden compassion for him. 'You look all in. Come home with me. I've some good whisky and a new Youssou N'Dour CD.'

He smiled. 'I guess that's an offer I can't refuse.'

———

With Jonas as pillion, Fela rode her bike south along the coast road to Dalkey. She slowed her speed as they entered the High Street and pulled up outside a bar next to the ruined remains of the old castle. They parked the bike and went inside. The bar was packed and noisy, so they went in search of somewhere quieter. It was a clear evening. Stars were already appearing in the sky, though it wasn't yet dark, so they kept walking until they reached the sea.

At the cliff edge they leaned their arms against the cold railing, gazing out over the water where a crescent moon gently floated. On the strand below a couple of people were taking the evening air with their dogs running in wild circles as if blown on the wind. The only sounds were the occasional bark muffled by the sound of waves, and the cries of a night bird from the woods above.

Fela shuddered and Jonas put an arm around her shoulder. 'Cold?'

'I was thinking of Simon. Why didn't he tell us how bad it was?'

'He always thought he could go it alone.'

She was silent for a moment. 'D'you think his death was an accident?'

'What d'you mean?'

'D'you think someone thought he was planning to destroy his research and went after him?'

'How would anyone know what was on his mind? Even us!'

'There are so many coincidences.'

'He was angry and pissed. Most likely he drove off, not caring where he was going, and fell asleep at the wheel. That's no less hard to accept than some dreamt up mystery.'

She shook her head. 'None of it makes sense. One thing we know. They can now carry on with the sale, without fear of opposition.'

'There's Conrad. He knows the dangers.'

'Conrad's a manager, and managers are there to serve the interests of their company.'

If there was no one left who'd lift a finger to prevent the vaccine from being sold, Simon's death was not just tragic but worse, pointless.

'Let's go down to the beach,' she said. 'I want to take off my shoes and walk on the sand.'

———

In his office on Monday morning Conrad got up from his desk to get a glass of water. His head ached and his mouth was dry. He shouldn't have gone back to Estelle's and drunk whisky. Ending up in bed together was an even bigger mistake. He'd told himself it was just for old time's sake, but times had changed.

His thoughts turned to Weiss. In the phone call they'd just had, he'd vetoed any suggestion of an internal investigation into the disappearance of Simon's research, insisting on secrecy until they received the official report from the Garda. But the secret would soon be out, and Conrad was pretty sure whatever the Garda had to say would leave them none the wiser.

He decided to visit Simon's lab and talk to his assistant, Paul, who'd already been interviewed and sworn to silence by Weiss. Paul was sitting in the centre of an empty lab, staring at the blank screen of his computer in a state of apparent despair.

'We can start by searching for any records, backup disks – anything relating to your research.'

'There's no point,' Paul said gloomily. 'It's all gone!'

'We don't know till we've looked. There must be something. Notes, for example, or records from the previous researcher.'

Reluctantly Paul joined in the search and they spent the morning going through files and cabinets, anywhere where material relating to the vaccine might be stored. They even searched the fridges, hunting for any trace that might have escaped detection. The few records they found related to experiments carried out in the project's earliest stages by Dr Murphy, and offered small hope of reconstruction. Simon had done a thorough job.

It was after six when Conrad returned to his office, and the light was going. The weary prospect of the rest of the week spent waiting for police evidence and doing his best to stave off Weiss called for distraction. He remembered the following evening was Tomas's gallery opening, and decided to give him a call in case he needed help installing the work. Tomas accepted his offer gladly, and as he finished the call his phone rang again.

'Conrad, it's Fela. I wondered if you're free for a drink this evening?'

Meeting Fela, he'd decided, was something best avoided until he could offer some comfort. He'd made sure she had plenty to do, since that was what she'd asked for. But he hadn't told her about Simon destroying his research. If he delayed much longer, she'd hear it through the grapevine, and that would be worse.

'Yes, that would be nice,' he said with slightly forced cheerfulness. 'I've just arranged to help Tomas in the gallery, but I should be done in a couple of hours. We could meet there: Optimum Art Works in Castle Street.'

'Okay. Eight-ish?'

'See you then.'

———

Tomas was shifting heavy sculptures around in the confined gallery space. For a moment, his tall figure in dusty white overalls reminded Conrad of an army captain with whom he'd struck up a brief friendship in Senegal. His own group had been sent in to help repel Al Qaeda rebels, who after the Algerian conflicts of the 1990s had spread south as far as Mali. The captain had been killed in an ambush while trying to free a village, a fate that might well have been Tomas's without his talent and good fortune.

'You're here!' Tomas said as he entered the gallery. 'Bella and I need help with the Elephant's Child. It won't fit the space, so we're going to have to put it on its own in the annex.'

The three of them set to work shifting the huge sculpture onto a rolling platform and wheeling it through to the annex. With the aid of levers, they manhandled it onto the plinth that had been prepared, then stood back breathing heavily. The form was split into two, reminiscent of a Henry Moore figure, and depicted a child or perhaps a lover reaching up towards the beloved.

'Magnificent!' Conrad said.

'Believe me, Tomas, this show's going to really put you on the map!' Bella said.

Back in the main room Conrad made a round of the rest of the pieces and the drawings that hung on the walls.

'Let's go eat,' said Tomas.

'Tell me where you're going, and I'll join you later. I'm meeting Fela, my assistant. There's been a disaster at work.'

Tomas, preoccupied, didn't complain.

'I've made up a guest list for tomorrow,' said Bella. 'Is there anyone you'd like to add?'

'Estelle Lanvier, from University College.'

'Give me her email. I'll send her an invite.'

The doorbell rang and Tomas went to answer it. 'Your colleague's here, Conrad!' he called out.

Fela entered the room and gazed about her in awe. She knew very little about sculpture, and certainly no artists apart from her father's musician friends. But the power of these pieces filled her with excitement.

She turned to Tomas. 'Can I come back later and take a proper look?'

'Please do! Best after the opening though, when there's no one here.'

'There'll be crowds everyday!'

He bowed in response to her compliment and reached for his coat.

'Your friend's a genius!' she said, when Tomas and Bella had gone.

Conrad smiled. 'It's not what you expected?'

'I'm not sure what I expected.' She searched for the right words. 'They speak so powerfully of Africa. Feelings and memories I'd forgotten, or maybe never knew I had.'

'That's what art can do.'

F ifteen minutes later they entered a bar known as The Library, chosen by Conrad for its quiet air of a gentleman's club, with bookshelves, leather armchairs and an open fire. They chose a corner, sat down and ordered drinks from the waiter.

'They do light meals too, if you're hungry.'

She shook her head and the waiter left.

'Do you have something particular you want to talk to me about?' Conrad asked after a brief pause.

She raised her gaze to his. 'Will there be an investigation into Simon's death?'

'First we need the report from the Garda.' He must tell her now, before things went any further. 'There's something you should know.'

She stiffened, in anticipation of another blow.

'When he left his lab, Simon took all his research with him – samples, hard drives, everything. We don't know what he did with it all, or whether he still had it with him when he crashed.'

She took a moment to digest this. 'You think someone knew what he'd done and followed him?'

'It's possible. The police say they found nothing in the car.'

'Either way, it's murder!'

'The guards believe his death was an accident.'

'So they're not going to do anything about it! Are you prepared to leave it at that?'

He shrugged. It was too soon, he judged, to tell her about the marks he'd seen on Simon's car.

'We have no evidence about whether or not he had the stuff with him. He could have hidden it somewhere.'

She tossed her head in exasperation. 'I gave Sean's death the benefit of the doubt, against every gut feeling. This time I'm not letting it go.'

'I understand your anger, but there's no connection whatsoever.'

'The company's the connection.'

'And you think someone in the company's responsible for both your father's and Simon's deaths? It makes no sense. They're the ones who lose out if they lose their chief researcher.'

'Not if they stole back his work first.'

'Whatever happened, we'll get nowhere by kicking up a stink. It needs careful handling. Believe me, as soon as I've something to go on, I'll act.'

'So I'm just to leave it to you?'

'For the moment.'

She went quiet. 'I think I'll go. I'm not in the best mood tonight.'

She stood up, leaving her barely touched glass on the table.

'Let me at least see you home.'

She shook her head. 'I've got my bike.'

A couple of people's eyes followed her as she walked to the door. Conrad finished his drink and signalled to the waiter for his bill. He understood Fela's anger, even while he feared for what she might do next. She was battling with too much grief and misfortune, and he had no idea how to comfort her. Perhaps Jonas could prove a better friend, because he was all she had left. He placed a couple of notes on top of the bill the waiter had left on the table, and got up.

———

The gallery was filling rapidly. The exhibition had received excellent previews in two of the main dailies, which guaranteed a good crowd in addition to the gallery's loyal clientele. The wine flowed, and when space became too crowded people spilled outside into the mild night. Seeing the event was such a success, one drink and Conrad would be on his way.

He noticed Estelle standing near the entrance and pushed through the crowd to greet her.

'Glad you could make it!'

'Your friend's the hottest thing in town!'

'You must come back when you can get a proper view of the work.'

'I intend to. Still, now I'm here I'd like a look round.'

'Let me show you The Elephant's Child. It's my favourite.'

They made their way through the gabbling people towards the annex.

Fela entered with Jonas. A voice from behind spoke her name and she turned to find herself face to face with Tomas.

'Glad you could make it! Get a drink, if you can move in this melee!''

He gestured towards a small bar on the far side of the room. He was expansive in a way she hadn't seen him before.

'So many people! You're putting Africa firmly on the artistic map!'

He smiled. 'I'll be here all day tomorrow, if you care to stop by. I need all the sincere criticism I can get!'

'Tomorrow I can't, but Saturday for sure.'

'And your friend?' He turned to Jonas.

'You'll have to ask him. He's also from Africa.'

'Cape Town. Though I haven't been back in a while.'

'You should. Things are changing all the time, though not always for the better, you may think.'

The two young men smiled at one another, and for a moment it was as if they shared some unspoken pact. It occurred to her that Jonas, so protective of his privacy even with those he considered friends, might prefer men. It was strange how little one knew even about those one considered close.

'There are too many people!' she said, when Tomas had moved on.

'You want to leave already?'

She nodded. 'Stay, if you like. I'll see you in the morning.'

Before Jonas could reply, she was gone.

S he parked her bike outside her house and walked in the direction of the small harbour for private boats. Feelings of grief and loneliness almost choked her. Hardly aware of where she was going, she found herself approaching the café bar where she went for breakfast sometimes on Sunday mornings. She and Maeve, the woman who ran it, had struck up a friendship. Maeve was tall, with pale Celtic skin, dark curly hair, and eyes of gooseberry green. At weekends she was helped out by her teenage son and daughter, and an elderly man, no doubt another relative and a bit slow, who worked in the kitchen. He made the breakfasts while she cooked a dish of the day and a pudding, and there was always a posy of flowers or leaves on each table brought in from Maeve's garden. At quiet times when there were few customers and Fela was alone, she came over and they sat together and talked.

This evening was busy, but Fela found a small table in the corner and sat down. People around her were chatting and laughing, but being amongst strangers with a book for company gave her the ease she sought.

By eleven, most people had left. Fela ordered a whisky, which Maeve brought to the table, together with the bottle and another glass for herself.

'So, what are you doing here on your own tonight?' Maeve asked. 'No Simon or Jonas?'

'Simon's had an accident.'

'I'm sorry to hear that. How's he doing?'

She hesitated. 'Actually, he's dead.'

'Oh dear Lord! And so soon after your da!' Maeve reached for her hands. 'You poor girl!'

'It's nice to be here, amongst people.'

'Ay, well, you're welcome any time, for a drink or a chat. Any time at all.'

'That means a lot!' Fela fought back tears.

'Here's to you!' Maeve raised her glass and Fela did likewise, comforted by her friend's warmth and the fiery spirit.

———

After dinner, Conrad dropped Estelle off at her flat and drove home. He refused her invitation of a nightcap, on the excuse that Tomas had invited him to join a group of his friends, though he was in no mood for either.

As he drove, he found himself thinking about the book Estelle had been reading in the bar the other night, *Biopiracy*. There was nothing particularly striking about a professor of biochemistry reading such a book, but Estelle was a political animal through and through. Her commitment to the national cause had once motivated her to work for the Agency, until that changed with the Iraq war and she'd grown increasingly critical of the Bush/Blair alliance. Eventually she'd quit the Agency for academia, but he couldn't help wondering whether, with her insatiable curiosity and talent for sniffing out conspiracies and shady deals, she retained a connection with her former employers. He'd also noticed the interest she took in the activities of his own company, partly accounted for by her fondness for her ex-student.

At home he resisted the whisky bottle and made himself a green tea, then put on a CD of Schubert Piano Impromptus and settled down in the living room. He loved this room, with the moonlight reflecting off the sea and the cries of sea birds through the open window. He felt his body relax and grow weightless, as though entering a peaceful void. It was a technique he'd learned from an old Chinese man in Dar es-Salaam, who ran a stall in the market selling herbal remedies. With Conrad's minimal knowledge of Swahili, the old man had managed to teach him to take the remedies in conjunction with certain meditative exercises to increase their effectiveness that had seen him through a host of stressful situations.

The telephone rang, and for a while he resisted answering, but it was impossible to ignore and he got up to answer. Chief Inspector Mulligan from the Garda Station in Wicklow apologised for calling so late but he was about to go on leave, he said, and wanted to inform him personally before he went. After thorough investigation they were satisfied Simon's death was an accident, the result of falling asleep at the wheel and losing control of the car. No further evidence of suspicious circumstances had come to light or witnesses been forthcoming, so they would be terminating the investigation. The coroner was expected to confirm their verdict, and he hoped this would put an end to any doubts.

Calling so late, even if the man was off on holiday,

struck Conrad as unusual. But the police worked odd hours, and no doubt he wanted to clear his desk before leaving. He wondered how he would tell Fela, and at that thought the calm of his meditative state evaporated. He knew well what the verdict would do to her.

———

O n Monday he arrived at the office early. His doubts were far from resolved, but except for the photo he'd taken of the dent at the rear side end of Simon's car, he had nothing to go on. As soon as he heard Fela arrive, he went into her room to tell her of the phone call he'd received from the Wicklow Garda. She heard him out with unexpected calm.

'So what do we do now?'

'I'll go down to Wicklow and pick up his things. I need to speak to Weiss first.'

He thought she'd say she wanted to come with him. Instead she asked, 'Does Jonas know?'

'I'll tell him.'

'I'll go.'

And before he could reply she was out of the door and disappeared down the corridor.

He returned to his room. Her response confused him, though he wasn't sure how else he could have broken the news. Simon was gone, and with him, it appeared, Fela's trust. R and D was a shambles, and it was his responsibility to deal with it, though he had little idea what to do next.

He picked up the phone to speak to Paul. 'Any progress?'

'I'm afraid not.'

'Keep trying. I'll be down shortly.'

The least he could do was provide him with some kind of assistance, though finding someone wouldn't be easy. Jonas was now his senior researcher, but his expertise lay in a wholly different area.

———

As soon as Fela opened the door to his lab, Jonas got up and grabbed his jacket.

'Fancy a quick coffee? I was just going.'

The canteen was almost empty, and they found a table near the window.

'I've been thinking about Simon's missing hard drives,' Fela said, as she sat down. 'Seeing how angry he was, has it occurred to you he might have destroyed them himself?'

'It's possible. That way he'd make sure the stuff would never be sold.'

'Perhaps whoever rammed his car didn't know and thought he had them with him. Which still makes it murder.'

'If that's so, how will we ever find out?'

'One way would be if the vaccine is offered for sale.'

'That could only be done through the black market, which is pretty secret.'

'Estelle has contacts. She might hear something.'

'So probably does Conrad. They share them from way back.'

'I'd rather not involve him.'

'Why not?'

'He represents Weiss, and his loyalty is to the company.'

When she got back to her office it was mid-morning, and Conrad was not there. He'd left a note on her desk saying he'd gone to Wicklow to make arrangements for bringing back Simon's body to the funeral parlour, and wouldn't be back in the office until the following day. That gave her the opportunity to carry out an idea she'd had of persuading Maloney, the chief caretaker, to let her look at the CCTV footage from the night of Simon's disappearance. It might show him leaving the building, and whether he was carrying anything bulky. If she waited until the end of the day when everyone else had gone home, she'd have a chance to get him alone.

The telephone rang in Conrad's office and she went to answer it.

'Could I speak to Dr Dreyer, please.'

She recognised Estelle's voice. 'He's out of the office until tomorrow. Can I take a message, Dr Lanvier?'

'Ah, Fela! His mobile's switched off but it's okay, I'll leave a message.' She rang off.

Simon used to speak about Estelle in a manner bordering on hero worship, which had always irritated her. But if anyone knew what he'd been planning, it would be her. Fela could ask her to meet up for a drink. It would be quite natural to want to talk about Simon.

———

I t was a little after six when she went down to Maloney's office. One wall of his room was filled with a bank of screens, each targeting a different part of the building. He made a point of remembering names and greeting every employee, and they were on friendly terms. She thought it best to ask him out straight if he'd let her go through the CCTV footage, to find out what Simon had been doing during his last hours in the building that final night.

'He's my oldest friend. I can't let him go without knowing how he was feeling when he drove off to his death,' she said.

Maloney was sympathetic. 'Officially I can't give you permission, but come back tomorrow around this time. I'll find the relevant footage and you can look through and see if it helps.'

'You're a real pal, Jim!'

She was disappointed not to be able to see it immediately, but 24 hours wasn't long to wait.

O n her way out to the car park, she called Estelle and arranged to meet her at the Library Bar of the Central Hotel, where she'd already been with Conrad.

When she arrived, Estelle was seated next to the fire, reading. Fela thought how sure of herself she looked in her concentration, as though surrounded by some impenetrable force field. She glanced up as Fela approached, closed her book and smiled.

'What would you like to drink? The house wines here are excellent.' She gestured to the waiter.

'A glass of house red then.'

The waiter left. Fela took off her coat and draped it over the back of her armchair.

'This is nice!'

'Dublin's best kept secret.' Estelle paused. 'I expect you've come to talk about Simon. It's devastating. For all of us, but especially you and Jonas.'

'Yes.'

'With sudden death the person becomes even more present in a way. In one's dreams.'

Fela nodded. 'Yes. Though I'm not doing much sleeping.'

The waiter returned and placed two glasses of red wine and a dish of nuts in front of them.

'You know Simon wasn't ready to put his vaccine out into the world, something the company refused to accept,' Fela said.

'I heard so.'

'You probably also know his research is missing. It's possible he had his hard drives with him at the accident, though so far nothing's been found.'

'So what d'you think I can do?'

'You have contacts in the pharmaceutical world. If someone has got hold of them and plans to sell, you might get to hear of it.'

Estelle smiled. 'My dear, you credit me with far more influence than I have. The world of industrial espionage is intensely secretive, resistant to any attempt at infiltration.'

Fela blushed, realising how naïve she must sound.

'Still if I do hear anything, be assured I'll tell you, and also Conrad,' Estelle said more kindly.

'A buyer had already been found and a sale agreed. They might still be interested.'

'I'll bear that in mind.'

There seemed little more to say on the matter, so she changed the subject.

'There was something else. Would you be prepared to speak at Simon's funeral? I know it's what he'd have wanted.'

Estelle smiled with genuine warmth. 'I'd be happy to. Tell me what kind of ceremony you want this to be.'

———

The following morning, Conrad was already in his office when Fela arrived. She took her time hanging up her coat and opening up her computer before knocking and entering. He was on the telephone and gestured to her to take a seat. He concluded the call and rang off. 'You look tired. Are you sleeping?'

'Not much.'

He looked exhausted himself, the lines on his face more deeply etched. 'The funeral's on Friday at Newlands Cross Cemetery,' he said. 'It's nice there as these places go, modern and more geared to cremations.' He paused. 'Did you manage to get hold of Simon's parents?'

'I've tried. His mother died of a heart attack a couple of years back and his father's always been a bit of a recluse, especially since her death. I've called and called but there's no reply and no answer machine. I also wrote a letter but so far no response. I don't know what else to do.'

'Well, I guess nobody will be wanting a full Mass.'

'Certainly not.' She hesitated. 'Did you see him?'

'Yes. He looked... peaceful.'

'Whenever I think of him, he's eager, impatient, or concentrating. Never peaceful.'

He nodded. 'If you want to go to the funeral parlour...'

She shook her head. 'Best to remember him as he was.' She hesitated. 'I asked Estelle. She said she'd be happy to speak at the funeral.'

'Good. We need to decide what sort of ceremony. Music as well as speakers, whatever you and Jonas would like.'

'I'll speak to him and give you a list.'

She returned to her office. The thought of Simon being put into a box and consigned to the flames was unbearable, but no more so than going into the ground to be slowly consumed by worms. Death's arbitrary power must be accepted, but there would be no solemnity. Live musicians would play him to the flames, and friends would speak of his laughter and stubbornness and many contradictions. She thought of his boyish smile and ready humour, masking a will she'd often called mulish, and with the thought came a momentary feeling of peace. She laid her head on her folded arms and fell asleep at her desk.

She was woken by Conrad entering her room. She sat up, rubbing her arms, which had gone to sleep with the awkwardness of her position.

'Dr Weiss and I have decided to put Paul, Simon's

assistant, in charge of recovering whatever's possible of the vaccine,' he said.

'No time wasted then!'

'I'm afraid not. Weiss is determined to press ahead, and Paul seemed the best man for the job. The only one, in fact.'

'The jaws of Mammon must be fed!' she returned brightly.

She stayed in her office until everyone had left at the end of the day and the building had grown quiet. At a quarter to seven she took the lift down to Maloney's room. He was expecting her and asked if she'd like a cup of tea, or perhaps a beer. She thanked him and said tea would be good. One of the CCTV screens was blank, ready for rerunning the footage concerning the hours between 8pm and midnight on the Friday evening she'd requested. The rest had to be left on. He showed her how to run the machine and went into the small adjoining kitchen to make tea.

First she concentrated on Simon's corridor. At around 8pm one person could be seen locking up his lab and walking to the lift, otherwise it remained empty. Eventually at just before ten she spotted Simon walking from the lift in the direction of his lab. He unlocked the door and entered, leaving it half open so that he could still be seen moving in and out of shot until the door slammed shut. She continued to watch when suddenly the screen went blank, then eventually the image reappeared. She ran back to the point where the camera cut out and checked the timing. Ten minutes had elapsed until the image returned, and there was no sign of Simon.

Jim returned with two mugs of tea. 'Any luck?'

'I picked him up going into his lab around ten. Then for some reason the camera cut out. I want to make sure when he left the building.'

'It does that sometimes. Maybe we can pick him up at the main entrance.'

Jim went to the screen that showed the foyer and entrance doors and set the time code. Fela fast-forwarded through almost an hour of footage, but there was no sign of Simon.

'Is there any other way out?'

'Only the basement exit, but that's locked on a time code.'

The phone rang and Jim went to answer it. It was his wife, and Fela assumed the call wouldn't be short. She sat for a moment trying to order her thoughts. Simon's accident had happened just after midnight, therefore he must have left his lab before eleven, around the time when the camera on his corridor cut out. She returned to the images of the foyer and ran through the footage, slowly this time. At 10.18 the footage counter suddenly jumped to 10.25. A casual observer might not have noticed, since there was no blank screen and no movement within the image to suggest a break in continuity. But her eyes were fixed on both image and counter. Two pieces of CCTV footage had disappeared, and it seemed too much of a coincidence to be accidental. She fished a notebook out of her bag and jotted down the exact time references of the missing sequences, then switched off the recorder and stood up.

'Thanks, Jim!' she mouthed to him, still on the phone. He gestured goodbye as she left the room.

———

The sun had disappeared behind the Wicklow hills, leaving streaks of yellow and duck egg blue in the darkening sky. She picked up her bike from the car park and drove back towards Dún Laoghaire. A couple of miles before reaching home, she pulled up at her favourite spot along the coast. It was a mild evening with almost no wind and the sea was calm. She kicked off her boots and walked along the strand, relishing the cold shock of the sand under her bare feet.

Her mind returned to the blank footage on the CCTV screen. Though Simon with his fierce rationality would tell her not to look for conspiracies where there were none, she didn't believe it was a coincidence. He was gone now, and all that mattered was to see his work wasn't exploited against his will. If he'd managed to destroy his hard drives, he could rest in peace. But if not, and if he'd been carrying anything when he left the building, it would have shown up on camera. She needed to find out what had become of it.

She walked back to her bike; reluctant to go straight home, she pulled out her mobile phone and called Jonas. When the call went to answerphone, she left no message. She was barely ten minutes from Conrad's house. If he was there, she might drop by for a quick drink. She dialled his number. It was picked up after a couple of rings.

'Yes?'

'Hi, it's Fela.'

'Everything okay?'

'Fine.' She hesitated. 'Are you busy?'

'Not particularly. I'm at home.'

'Is Tomas there?'

He gave a brief laugh. 'No. He's in town.'

'Can I come by for a quick drink? I'm just around the corner.'

'Of course.'

'See you in a few minutes.'

As she drove the short distance to his house, she wondered if she'd done the right thing, but it was too late now.

———

The blinds over the huge window of the living room were as usual undrawn, and bright stars appeared in the sky. Conrad picked up an open bottle of red wine from the low table and offered her a glass. 'I don't usually drink alone, but it's a while since I've had an evening at home.'

'And now I'm here to disturb the peace.'

'Is there a reason?'

She smiled. 'It's a beautiful night and I wasn't sleepy.'

He observed her as she sipped her wine. 'Has something happened? You seem different.'

'Different?'

'Calmer.'

'I'm trying to focus on what to do now, rather than dwelling on the past.'

He reached forward to refill his glass. 'Do you have a problem with Tomas?'

'What an odd question!'

'When you called, you asked if he was here.'

'Maybe at first. He makes me understand how little I know about my African roots.'

'I doubt that concerns him. Like most artists, he's obsessive and that can make him seem arrogant.'

'He's certainly talented. Have you known him long?'

'Four or five years. We met via a mutual friend in Nairobi. He had an exhibition there, and I offered to put him up if ever he came to Ireland. Since then he's been living in France. He had a show a few months ago at the Maeght Foundation near Nice, and I went to see it.'

She'd never imagined Conrad having artistic interests; rather a man focused on profit, like every other company manager.

'We work together every day, yet I know so little about you.'

'What d'you want to know?'

She shrugged. 'Why you're here? What this job means to you?'

'What does any job mean? A way to earn a living.'

'Is that all? Is working for an international pharma company at the cutting edge of research a source of pride, or also of concern?'

'It seemed like an interesting challenge. I'm not sure I've a simple answer to your question.'

She hesitated for a moment. 'D'you still like what you do?'

'I neither like nor dislike it. But I realise I've got even less room for manoeuvre than I thought.'

'And that matters?'

'Yes.'

'So what will you do about it?'

'That indeed is the question.'

She waited for him to elaborate but he said no more. 'Off the record, how possible do you think it will be to salvage the vaccine?'

'Off the record? Impossible.'

'So why play along with Weiss's fantasy?'

A look of weariness passed across his face. He hadn't expected an inquisition. 'I could say, it's to gain time for developing some other product that will stop the company from pulling out of Ireland and be of real use to the world. I'm sorry if that sounds thin.'

'No, it doesn't.' She paused. 'Are there other things in the pipeline?'

'Nothing so far that will bring in the same profit. The company's future doesn't particularly matter to me, but it does to a lot of others. If they pull out, those people won't find it easy to get equivalent jobs in the present climate.'

She walked over to the window and gazed out to sea. After a moment or two she turned back to face him. 'I looked at the CCTV footage from the night of Simon's accident. I was searching for signs of him entering or leaving his lab and whether he was carrying anything.'

'And what did you see?' Conrad was all attention.

'I saw him enter his lab around ten. Then something odd happened. The image went blank.'

'How long for?'

'About ten minutes. I also checked through footage of the main entrance for nearly an hour to see if I could catch him leaving the building. Again there was a gap of around seven minutes, but no sign of Simon. He appears to have vanished.'

'Did you ask Maloney about the blank bits?'

'He said the camera must have been faulty. Sometimes they cut out for no reason. I don't think he'd noticed the second gap. Unless, of course, someone ordered him to remove the footage.'

Conrad poured himself another glass of wine. 'Could you have missed him?'

'I watched it until after eleven. If he'd left after that, he couldn't have had the accident at midnight.'

He went to refill her glass, but she covered it with her hand.

'I'm on the bike.'

'I'll need to take a look.'

'Only don't say I spoke to you. Maloney might get into trouble for letting me see it.'

'Of course.'

She picked up her jacket. 'I'd better go.'

'I was going to offer you something to eat.'

'Another time! I need to go home and sleep.'

He accompanied her into the hall. At the front door she reached forward and kissed him on the cheek, then turned quickly and disappeared into the night.

———

J onas turned on the TV. A Breakfast News Channel interviewer was discussing the consequences of the global banking crisis with the Irish Finance minister. After a few minutes he switched off. He had little time for politics or politicians. The banks had been deregulated, and now people were bearing the consequences of their reckless greed. A man-made accident in which, as usual, those responsible would be the last to bear the brunt.

He put his cereal bowl and coffee cup in the sink, then carefully spread the shirt he'd hand-washed over the drying rack to avoid ironing. Simon enjoyed ironing, saying he found it soothing and liked the smell. To Jonas it was just an irritating chore. It was impossible to take in the shock of Simon no longer being there. He'd heard Weiss was planning to contact his predecessor, Dr Murphy, to come in and work with Paul, though the chances of them salvaging anything seemed zero. He hadn't shared Simon's hard-line attitude, and mostly he'd kept his thoughts to himself, knowing his opinion would make little difference. In his view, neutralising any harmful side effects of the vaccine was surely possible and might have been done relatively quickly, at least to conform to current safety standards. It was an accepted fact no one ever knew for certain what the results would be until a drug had been tested on the people it was intended for, which could take years. But for Simon that risk was unacceptable.

It wasn't the first time they'd differed over some ethical issue. Simon, for example, declared all whites to be fundamentally racist, and that offended Jonas deeply.

Raised in Devon where he'd scarcely encountered a black face, what did Simon know about racism! Jonas had kept quiet about his past, unwilling to expose precious childhood memories to an onslaught of derision. He didn't deny the brutality of the apartheid regime, but neither could he erase the joys he'd known. His parents had been farmers, his mother from Boer stock, living a hand-to-mouth existence in a remote region, toiling alongside their black workers in relative harmony. Jonas ran wild with the native boys who were his only friends, picking up their language, listening to their songs and stories and sharing their food. Then when he was ten, his uncle on a neighbouring farm was hacked to death by his workers and, though Jonas never denied the crimes and injustices committed by whites, the fear this brutal event instilled never left him. Later at university, he'd done his best to ignore the past with its impossible moral dilemmas, and on receiving his degree he left the country, unlikely to return.

He felt almost no African connection with Fela, despite her mother being from Jo'burg. Born and raised in England, she seemed to him entirely British. But meeting Tomas had revived for a moment an unaccustomed feeling of nostalgia, a longing to recover a connection to the siren voices from the world he'd turned his back on.

———

He arrived at the company building ahead of most of the workforce, and went straight to Simon's lab. The door was locked, but he could hear someone moving about inside. He knocked and after a moment Paul opened it.

'Can I help you?'

'I heard you'd been put in charge of recovering whatever can be salvaged of Simon's and your research. Is there anything I can do? Can I come in for a minute?'

Reluctantly Paul stood aside for him to enter.

'What can anyone do? Everything's destroyed!' He gestured towards the empty fridge and blank screen of Simon's computer.

'I understand Dr Weiss has contacted Simon's predecessor.'

'Pointless!' Paul scoffed.

'It's not my field, but Simon and I were close colleagues.'

'So did he tell you what he was planning to do with nearly two years' hard work?' Paul asked aggressively.

'I'm afraid not.'

Jonas watched him unplug an extra hard drive from his computer and slip it into a small backpack on the floor next to his desk, then remove his lab coat and replace it with his anorak. He picked up his backpack and opened the door, waiting for Jonas to go through before pulling it to behind him and locking it.

'Can I buy you a coffee?' Jonas said, curious now why Paul seemed so eager to be rid of him.

'I'm going for breakfast. I was in early and I haven't eaten.'

'Perhaps I could come with you. I'd like to talk.'

'I'm not going to the canteen.' Paul quickened his pace.

Irritated by his rudeness, Jonas hurried to catch up

with him as he disappeared through the doors to the staircase. 'Hang on, mate! What's the hurry?'

Paul turned on him, openly hostile. 'I'm not your mate, and I don't need your interference!'

Paul started down the stairs, but Jonas grabbed him by the arm.

'What the hell's your problem?'

'Leave me alone!'

He pulled himself free and started to run down the stairs. Jonas, following, grabbed hold of his backpack. Paul twisted away from him and lost his footing; the two of them catapulted down the flight of concrete steps, landing in a heap at the bottom.

Jonas pulled himself up, shocked and bruised. Paul, on whom he had fallen, was groaning and in obvious pain. One strap of his backpack had snapped and the bag lay on the ground a couple of feet away. Jonas reached for it.

'Give me that!' Paul almost screamed.

Jonas held on to it. 'Are you badly hurt?'

Paul tried to get up and grab the bag but fell back to his knees with a cry of pain. 'Jesus! My ankle!'

Jonas bent down to help him up. 'Lean on me. We'll get you somewhere you can sit down, and I'll take a look at that ankle.'

Jonas shouldered the rucksack. Having no choice, Paul accepted his support and hopped painfully step by step through the connecting doors into the neighbouring corridor. They reached a bench next to the water cooler, and Paul sank down to rest. Jonas braced Paul's injured leg against his knee, and pulled up his trouser to examine the ankle. The skin was turning an angry red, and already it was starting to look puffy. Jonas turned his foot gently from side to side and Paul cried out in pain.

'It might be broken. You need to get it looked at.'

'Fuck you!' Paul groaned.

'I'll drive you to the hospital.'

He placed Paul's foot back on the ground and undid the laces on the sneaker that contained his swelling foot. Paul was shivering now, and Jonas pulled his anorak up around his shoulders that had half come off in his fall. While Paul wrestled his arm into the empty sleeve and struggled with the zip, Jonas turned to the water filter to fill a plastic cup. With Paul distracted, he quickly felt inside the backpack and his fingers closed over the hard drive. He slipped it out of the bag and hid it behind the water cooler, then turned back to Paul and handed him the cup.

'Can you make it to the lift?'

Paul nodded and took a sip. Jonas picked up his backpack. 'I'll carry this for you.'

This time Paul made no objection.

———

J onas returned from the hospital, picked up the key to Simon's old lab from the porter on duty, then went straight to the water cooler on the first floor to retrieve the hidden hard drive. Back at the lab, he unlocked the door and went over to Paul's computer. He connected the hard drive and tried various passwords scribbled down in a small notebook he'd found in the bag with the hard drive. Eventually he found one that worked, and stared at the screen in astonishment. There were notes and calculations documenting the various stages of development of the vaccine formula, culminating in Simon's latest version. At the end Simon had typed, 'THIS FORMULA CANNOT BE USED IN ITS PRESENT FORM!'

He sat back in his chair. Paul must have realised Simon was serious about destroying their work and secretly made a copy. But if he intended to sell the stuff himself, how would he find contacts? Any buyer, including the original, would balk at negotiating with someone who wasn't the representative of a recognised company.

He unplugged the hard drive then ran quickly through Paul's emails, looking for anything to do with setting up a meeting or some kind of negotiation. But there was nothing. Either he'd skilfully covered his tracks or, more likely, he hadn't yet started. The question was what he, Jonas, was going to do with the information. The most obvious thing would be to take the hard drive to Weiss, who would reopen the sale agreement and possibly reward him for his loyalty. Or he could do what Simon had intended and destroy it. But there was a third option. He could arrange a deal himself and make the fresh start he'd always dreamed of on the proceeds.

The thought was at first too shocking to contemplate. But it was also intriguing, both in its daring and its duplicity. All his life he'd lived under the shadow of those more brilliant and innovative than himself. Even the prize he'd received for his fertiliser owed more to his predecessor's efforts than his own. He didn't share Simon's mercurial intelligence, or Fela's sure instinct that rarely let her down. It would be a chance to do something extraordinary, something that mattered and would contribute to the common good. It would earn him the respect he craved.

————

P aul was confined to home, so the Herculean task of recovering whatever was possible of the vaccine formula seemed more hopeless than ever. At the end of another frustrating day, Conrad left his office and set off for home. As he entered his cottage the phone was ringing.

'I tried your mobile. It was switched off,' Estelle's voice said.

'I was driving.'

'Get hands free! I'll be with you in half an hour.'

'Can't it wait? I've had a filthy day.'

'No, it can't. I won't stay long.'

He cursed silently. Estelle was the last person he wanted to see right now.

In less than half an hour, her car pulled up outside and she was at the door.

'Sorry about the drama,' she said as he took her coat. 'I thought it best to speak to you in person.'

They entered the living room and she looked around her admiringly.

'This is nice! It's the first time I've been here.'

'Is that a reproach?'

'Well, I'd have liked an invitation. You've lived here over six months.'

'My apologies! Would you like a drink?'

'Please. Whisky.'

He went into the kitchen and returned with a bottle of Bushmills and two glasses. He poured a shot and handed it to her. 'Water?'

'No thanks.' She walked over to the window and gazed out.

'Fabulous view!'

'Tell me what you came for.'

She turned back into the room. 'It seems someone's offering your vaccine for sale.'

For a moment he was too dumbstruck to speak.

'I've just been informed.'

'By who?'

'Conrad, how long have we known each other? You know I can't reveal my sources.'

He made an impatient gesture. 'Whatever you're up to these days is no concern of mine. I just want to be sure this is genuine.'

'I wouldn't be bothering you if it wasn't,.'

'What evidence is there it's ours? There are plenty of spies around. Someone might have come up with something similar.'

'This is a small world. It's the same.'

He felt a profound sense of weariness. This business was never ending. He thought of what Fela had said about the CCTV footage cutting out. Simon must have been seen carrying out the hard drives. Either he'd hidden them where they'd been found, or they'd been stolen from his car at the time of the accident. He brought his attention back to Estelle and *Biopiracy*, the book she'd been reading in the bar the last time they'd met. It was a favourite with eco-warriors and their fellow travellers, and she'd always fancied herself a radical. It seemed likely her informant was one of them.

'Stealing industrial property and selling unlicensed products – they're both illegal!'

'That never stopped people.'

She reached for the bottle and poured herself another shot, then sat back in her chair. 'The question is, how far can I trust you?'

He shrugged. 'That's for you to decide.'

She paused briefly before deciding to continue. 'You'll need a go-between, someone who monitors these sorts of deals. I can make some inquiries. But no one, not even your young assistant, must know.'

'How come you're willing to take such a risk?'

'Being a professor doesn't mean I've abandoned all my principles. Simon did everything he could to stop his work from being misused, because he believed it was danger-ous. Let me know when you've made up your mind.'

When she had left, Conrad poured himself another whisky and thought about what she had said. Whoever was offering the vaccine for sale must have been aware of Simon's movements, which suggested it was someone from the company. He ran through the possible candi-dates. First up was Weiss. He might have set someone to keep an eye on Simon, in case he did something rash. But having got hold of the hard drive, he would surely have returned to the original deal. He wouldn't put the stuff out on the black market. Apart from him, there were Estelle, Jonas, Fela, and Paul, none of whom seemed remotely possible. Instinct warned him not to trust Estelle or her friends, but if he wanted information, he had no idea where else to turn.

He waited an hour or so until she would have reached home and dialled her number. She answered at once.

'I've been thinking over what you said. Can we meet tomorrow? I can come to the university, if that's good for you.'

'Best to meet in town. Usual place?'

'Okay. Six-ish.'

He opened up his laptop and began searching online for information about movements concerned with anti-globalisation and biopiracy. He was surprised to find how widespread and well organised they were. He'd expected a loose collection of anarchists and professional protesters. Instead he found a range of international journalists, academics, and even some distinguished public figures, all of whom presented formidable arguments against unfettered capitalism and the unchecked activities of the pharmaceutical companies. Instinct cautioned him against engaging with proselytisers of any kind, but curiosity drove him on.

The following morning he heard Fela enter her office, and a few minutes later she tapped at his door. He noticed with sudden tenderness how drawn she looked. Despite that, she reminded him of what a fellow legionnaire had once said about his small daughter: 'C'est une force de la nature!' That was Fela - a force of nature.

'So, what's on the agenda today?' she said with slightly forced cheerfulness.

'I'm meeting Weiss to talk about plans for the future.'

'D'you have any new ideas?'

'There's exciting work being done on bioelectronics. Eventually they'll be used to treat a vast range of chronic diseases, and we don't want to be left behind. We also need to go through research proposals from the last couple of years, find out which went on to production and how well they've done. Oh, and any job applications that are worth a second look.'

She lingered a moment longer. 'It's Simon's funeral on Friday. I wondered if you're planning to speak? I'm finalising the order of service.'

'Of course. I hadn't forgotten.'

'I've drawn up a list of music and some of his favourite readings.'

'I'll probably just say a few words. The rest is best left to you. I'm sure you'll do it perfectly.'

———

He left his office at six and arrived first for his meeting with Estelle. She'd texted that the people she knew had already taken up the cause of the vaccine, so he'd be forced into collaboration with them whether he liked it or not. So far it appeared there was no evidence of industrial espionage, or that Simon had willingly entrusted his work into someone else's keeping, and his death remained a mystery.

Estelle came in and sat down.

'Sorry to keep you waiting.' The waiter appeared at her side. 'A glass of your house red, please.'

'It gave me time to think. I'm curious about these people you mentioned.'

She smiled at him. 'I know what you're thinking. These fanatics Estelle's involved with. They're not to be trusted.'

'Something like that.'

'Well, for a start the people I know are rational and responsible. They're committed to exposing the dirty deals companies like yours try to get away with. The fight isn't against governments. It's against injustice and corruption world-wide. The methods they use are mostly legal.'

'There are extremists in every organisation.'

'Of course.'

'Still, I'm here. Despite my scepticism.'

She nodded her thanks as the waiter placed a glass on the table and disappeared.

'Whoever's offering this stuff for sale is most likely an amateur acting on his own behalf for a single pay-off,' she said. 'That means he or she should be easy to track down.'

'Does your contact have any idea how they got hold of the material?'

'They assume they knew Simon and his movements.'

No one Conrad could think of would be capable of following Simon, coldly ramming his car then making off with the stuff. But hiring someone else to do the job would take money and contacts: no ordinary person could do that.

'If you get a name, please let me know.'

'Of course.'

He drained his glass. 'I noticed the book you were reading the other day – *Biopiracy*. Have you converted to their cause, or are you just an interested bystander?'

She paused for a moment. 'I was in Tanzania a few months ago. A well-known antibiotic with a shelf life of not more than six months in the tropics was being sold two years after its normal sell-by date, at ten times the official price. In Colombia, the mark-up for similar products has been reported as 6000 per cent. Banned or unlicensed drugs with known side-effects are being sold every day to pregnant women and children all over the third world. They route the drugs through countries which require no registration; they're banned for use in the countries where they're manufactured. Your vaccine is part of this trade. Do we simply turn a blind eye?'

'Did you talk to Simon about this?'

'Briefly. He found an article lying around in my office and wanted to know more.'

'And you told him where to look.'

'The internet's open to everyone.'

'And now he's dead.'

Her eyes flashed in anger. 'You think that has anything to do with me?'

'It's not totally unconnected.'

She returned her glass to the table. 'You may have no moral conscience, but others do. Find your scapegoat if you must, but don't lay your guilt at my door.'

She picked up her bag and stood up.

'Estelle! I'm sorry.'

'See you around!'

He watched her go, cursing himself for his crassness. He knew how touchy she was on issues she held dear. And she was right. The responsibility for Simon's death was his alone. Unlike Weiss, who believed morality went hand in hand with expediency, he'd kidded himself he could subvert the more harmful decisions while doing his bosses' bidding. Now he was forced to seek help from people he instinctively distrusted but needed their understanding of the murky world of international deals and subterfuge. Meanwhile there was a funeral to prepare for.

———

F ela gazed into her wardrobe. She wanted something colourful without being frivolous, to suit the vividness of Simon's short life. In the end she chose a dark red jacket over the blue linen dress he'd admired the last time she wore it. For the reading, she'd take a poem by Yeats. She loved it, especially for its final lines – 'O chestnut tree, great rooted blossomer, Are you the leaf, the blossom or the bole? O body swayed to music, O brightening glance, How can we know the dancer from the dance?'

The chestnut was her favourite tree. There'd been one in their garden in Battersea, in whose great branches she'd spent hours concocting potions in jam jars, reading, and observing the world from on high. Yeats's musical lines spoke of interconnectedness, even things as apparently different as the fragile blossom and stalwart trunk of the great tree. It was a thought dear to Simon. And then there was the dancer – precious human atom, ceaselessly whirling within the turning world.

But not all dances were expressions of life. She recalled the medieval fresco she'd once seen that encircled the walls of a small church in Northern France. There the dance was Death's, who with his bony finger and scythe led the villagers in a grotesque procession towards the waiting grave. In this vision everything was subject to His bitter power, and the dance was the exhausted frenzy of people marching to their doom. That no doubt was how things had seemed in the terrible years of the Great Plague, but not for Simon. His dance would not be Death's, but a defiant celebration of life.

Her phone rang. The car to take them to the crematorium was waiting. She grabbed her jacket, shoved her volume of poems into her bag, and left the house.

———

Crematoriums were a relatively new thing in Catholic Ireland, and Mount Jerome claimed to be the greenest in the country. The chapel was grey and undistinguished, surrounded by a massive graveyard. But off to one side there was a garden full of flowers, leading down to a river and shallow weir banked by trees. In the circumstances it was a pleasant place to be.

For a few minutes she and Jonas stood near the chapel entrance, greeting people they knew. The dark glasses he wore with his white shirt and sombre suit made him look like a gangster, and she suppressed an impulse to giggle. Weiss arrived accompanied by a couple of men also in dark suits, whom he introduced as having travelled from

Geneva. Then the hearse turned in through the cemetery gates.

As it made its solemn way towards them, Fela put her hand to her mouth to stop herself from crying out. It slowed to a halt, and six burly undertaker's men started to unload the coffin. It was made of wicker, as she and Jonas had requested, threaded with small bunches of spring flowers. The bouquets and wreaths had been placed outside the chapel for people to view as they exited, to be sent later to a neighbouring hospice.

She was hardly able to follow the ceremony. Conrad slipped in at the last minute and sat down behind her and Jonas. There were prayers, and they sang 'The Lord is my Shepherd,' then Weiss went to the lectern and made a speech about Simon's exceptional talents and his irreparable loss to the company, followed by a few heart-felt words from Estelle. They listened to the slow move-ment from Mozart's horn concerto that Simon had played as a schoolboy with the National Youth Orchestra. Jonas gave a short speech about his best friend that made people laugh, and then it was Fela's turn.

She got up and walked to the lectern, trying to clear her mind of everything save the words she would repeat, reminding herself to read slowly so not a syllable be lost. When she sat down, the audience was silent. Jonas rested his hand on her knee and whispered in her ear, 'Well done, d'Artagnan!' Finally, after a short blessing, everyone filed out to strains of Louis Armstrong singing 'What a Wonderful World'.

On her way to the exit door she paused beside the

coffin, and laid her hand on the wickerwork. Soon that familiar face would be consumed with the rest of his body in the purifying fire of the furnace, first the soft parts then the ribs, pelvis, heaviest bones, and last of all the skull, until only ash was left. She felt no horror. His body would be rendered into dust, and his spirit carried off with his ashes into the wind. She pulled a stem of bluebell from a bunch of flowers on the coffin and placed it in the buttonhole of her jacket. It would wilt soon, but that scarcely mattered.

Outside Weiss was directing people to a drinks reception, and into cars waiting to ferry them there. Fela turned aside, unable face the melee in which Jonas was already caught up. She felt a hand on her arm and turned round.

'Are you going to the wake?' Conrad said.

She shook her head, not trusting herself to speak.

'I've got the Jeep, if you'd like a lift somewhere?'

'The sea, perhaps,' she managed to get out. 'I'd like to walk for a bit.'

He nodded. 'It's this way.'

They drove along the coast in silence until they came to an inlet at the side of the road. Beside it, woods rose up to meet the sky, and on the far side a path led down to the strand.

'Is this a good place?'

She nodded.

'There's a rock at the top of this hill where I sometimes sit and look out over the sea.'

They took the steep path that zigzagged up through the trees, and emerged into the open. Bees thronged the gorse newly in bloom, whose scent filled the air. They left the path and made their way over brambles and hummocks of coarse grass, till they came to a slab of rock. Tiny wildflowers and tufts of moss grew in its crevices; its surface was polished smooth by weather and passers-by who chose it for a resting place. Conrad offered Fela his coat to sit on but she declined, relishing the feel of the stone's warmth. The wind had died down and the breeze brought a taste of the sea.

They sat for a while in silence, gazing out over the grey-green water. To their left was a small island, where she could see sheep grazing on the spring grass. They'd been brought over by boat and would remain there all summer. She envied the farmer's life that followed the rhythm of the seasons in unending rotation. Her own was without meaning or shape.

'Up here you could almost ride the sky like a bird,' Conrad said.

'That's why I love it.'

He paused. 'Will you stay, now Simon's gone?'

'I don't know. I came here as much for my father. Now they're both gone.'

She turned to face him. 'And you? You left the army to come here. Did you think then things would be so complicated?'

'I have to finish what I started. After that, who knows.'

'And how will you do that?'

'I'm not sure yet.'

She fell silent for a moment. 'Was Simon right, d'you think? That all we're doing is dumping pharmaceuticals on places caught up in an endless round of poverty and wars?'

Her words stung him. 'I wish I could give a simple denial.'

She paused. 'I'm sorry. I'm lousy company.'

She longed for some narcotic to annihilate the feelings that engulfed her. Sex was the best she knew, but she swiftly dismissed the idea. Whatever desire impelled her to reach out to Conrad for strength and warmth, it would only lead to more regrets and confusion.

She lay back against the rock, one arm folded behind her head. Gazing with half-closed eyes at passing clouds, her thoughts gradually quietened. She scarcely registered as he took hold of the hand that rested on her thigh, until she felt his mouth on hers. She closed her eyes and kissed him back. At length he pulled away.

'Let's go to my place,' he said, offering her his hand.

Without more words they descended the hill.

By the time they reached his house, her feeling of recklessness on the hilltop was receding. If she'd had her bike she'd have made some excuse and left.

'Would you like a drink? Coffee, or something stronger?' said Conrad.

'Whisky, if you have it.'

He hung up their coats and disappeared into the kitchen. She went into the living room and gazed out of the window at the sun-dappled water stretching to the horizon. She heard him come back, but didn't turn round. He placed a glass in her hand and she raised it to her lips, welcoming the burning sensation of the spirit. She felt him standing close behind her and tipped back her head until it rested against his chin. He smoothed the hair from her forehead and for a moment they remained as they were. Then she turned to face him.

'Come to bed,' he said softly.

She swallowed the rest of her whisky and placed the glass on the table.

In the bedroom she let her clothes fall in a heap on the floor and he drew her down onto the bed. His body was without softness, but had a suppleness that moulded itself to hers. At first she felt shy, as though making love with a stranger. But as one wave of pleasure succeeded another, she abandoned herself to the oblivion she sought.

Evening came on and the light outside faded. He got out of bed and went to the kitchen to prepare some supper, returning with a tray. They ate in bed with their fingers then made love again. At dawn she stirred, restless with still unsatisfied desire. He woke and took her in his arms, until finally exhausted they fell asleep again.

The next time she woke it was after nine and he was gone. She got up, showered, dressed quickly, and went into the kitchen. He was working on his laptop at one end of the table, where he'd laid out coffee, fresh rolls, honey and fruit.

'This looks good! But you shouldn't have let me sleep so long.'

'It's Saturday! Enjoy your breakfast. I have to meet Weiss and those guys from HQ. They go back this afternoon. If you're happy to wait, I won't be more than a couple of hours.'

She was about to agree when the door opened and Tomas appeared, bleary-eyed and wearing a long robe that served as a nightgown. Suddenly self-conscious, she drained the last of her coffee. 'I should be getting home.'

'Am I to take it personally, you running off as soon as I appear?' said Tomas.

'Of course not. There are things I need to do.'

'I'll drop you home,' said Conrad.

She shook her head. 'I'll enjoy the walk. It's only a couple of miles.'

Tomas sat down at the table and poured himself a coffee. 'Well, it's a fine day for it.' He smiled at her.

Conrad accompanied her to the hall.

'Thanks for seeing me though that ordeal yesterday!'

'I'm here whenever you want me.'

She reached forward and kissed him.

————

Jonas carried his clothes down to the communal basement of his apartment block where the laundry machines were kept. He did this every Saturday morning around eight, before most of the other inhabitants were up. He was thinking about the vaccine. The funeral had distracted him from the dilemma he faced, but now Simon was cremated he must decide what he was going to do.

He tipped his clothes into the machine, followed by two tablets of detergent, set the programme and switched it on. For a moment he stood staring at the glass porthole as the contents started to revolve. Paul obviously intended to sell the vaccine. He'd probably already made contacts. If Weiss got wind of it, he would seize the stuff back and make sure Paul got the punishment he deserved. Jonas could sit by and let these things happen, or do the deal himself, take the money and make his escape.

With the world running out of antibiotics, he'd dreamt for some years of finding a way to research how to combine modern with traditional methods of counteracting dangerous infectious diseases. Peru and Bolivia were the places he'd studied. With their rich variety of plants and trees used as medicines for thousands of years by indigenous people, they gave ample scope for discovering revolutionary remedies that were both effective and safe. It was now generally recognised that plants were a unique and underexploited source of bioactive compounds. He'd followed with interest research being done into how to combine complex plant extracts. There were big claims being made for some individual compounds, that could act either as stand-alone therapies or as adjuncts with other antibiotics to make them more effective, for example in the fight against MRSA. It was a rich field, and as the pharmaceutical companies ran out of options, even they had started to embrace it.

There would be problems, of course. Any such research would require drawing up watertight patents even before any trials were carried out, both to guard against the exploitation of native peoples and against destruction of the environment. All this would require considerable investment, and the sale of the vaccine could provide it. He'd need to start small, just himself and a couple of assistants who spoke the local language. His Spanish was more than adequate, since he'd spent several months in the Andes on his Ph.D research programme. As they made progress, they could take on more help from local experts and look for sponsorship from abroad. Once they had something to show, with world health in crisis raising further funds shouldn't be too hard.

The more he thought about it, the more what had seemed a mere pipe-dream was turning into a reality. But he'd need to act fast, and there was the problem of Paul. By now he'd have discovered his hard drive with the copies of the formula had gone, and Jonas had no idea how he'd react. He could offer him some kind of payment in recompense, even a share in the enterprise if he was prepared to invest the cash, which would ultimately be more financially rewarding. He'd heard he'd been released from hospital with his leg in a cast and was convalescing at home. He'd have to pay him a visit.

———

Paul lived with his sister in a flat in Stoneybatter, the same neighbourhood where Fela's father had his cottage. Jonas had never been to Sean's place and being unfamiliar with the area, it took him some time to find the address. He'd telephoned to make sure the sister was at work and Paul was alone. At first Paul refused to see him, but the offer of money had softened him up and in the end he agreed to a visit.

He found the street eventually and parked the car outside an old-fashioned gents' outfitters. Paul's flat was above it, with its own side entrance. He rang the bell and was buzzed in. The living room was stuffy, crammed with furniture and bric-a-brac, as though after the break-up of the family home nothing could be let go. Paul was sitting in an armchair, watching a TV quiz show.

'There's a beer in the fridge if you want one,' he said by way of greeting.

'Thanks. I'm fine. How are you feeling?'

Paul shrugged. 'As you'd expect with a shattered ankle.'

Jonas pulled a packet of the tobacco he knew Paul smoked from his pocket and laid it on the arm of his chair.

'Could we turn that down?' he said, indicating the TV.

Paul did so reluctantly, and Jonas took a seat opposite him.

'You know why I'm here.'

'I didn't think it was a social visit.' Paul's attention continued to be fixed on the TV screen.

'You blame me for your accident. But that's what it was, an accident. We both lost our footing and you got the worst of it. I'm truly sorry for that.'

Paul said nothing.

'You also know I've got your hard drive.'

This time Paul flashed him a look of open hostility. 'So you're going to tell me I'm a thief? Shop me to the authorities?'

'That's not why I came.'

'If I hadn't made those copies, the formula would be lost. It was my work as much as Eastlake's. So what's your claim?'

'The vaccine belongs to the company. Anyone else trying to sell it is breaking the law. We'd need good reason and a workable exit strategy.'

JANE CORBETT

Paul turned to face him. 'We? So what have you got in mind?'

Jonas ignored his sarcasm. 'I've a proposition.'

'Please, do enlighten me.'

'I want to set up a research group to look into how certain indigenous people use plants as medicines, to see what we can learn from them. With the world running out of antibiotics, pharmaceutical companies are more and more interested. Eventually it could be very profitable. With money from the sale of the vaccine we could make a start.'

'You're joking?'

'Not at all. Come to South America and see for yourself. There's not much future here. Have you ever been to that part of the world?'

'No, and I don't intend to.'

'In that case I'll give you some money from the sale straight away. If you invested in the project, of course, you'd end up a lot better off.'

'D'you know what I say to your proposition? I say, fuck you! You're out of your mind! You stole that hard drive from me, and I've no desire to be part of your hare-brained scheme. Frankly I don't see why I should share any money with you.'

Jonas fought to contain his temper. He was offering Paul a stake in a venture that could end up paying handsomely and make a significant contribution to medical research. 'Unfortunately the hard drive's in my possession.'

'I've already started negotiations.'

'Not much point when you've nothing to negotiate

with.'

'You really are a bastard! What's to stop me telling Weiss you copied the formula and are offering it for sale? My word against yours, and I know who he'll believe.'

'Or I can simply hand the hard drive over to him and you get nothing, except a conviction for stealing company property.'

'I'll see you in court for grievous bodily harm!'

'With no witnesses? You slipped, my friend. I did my best to save you and got you to hospital.'

They'd reached an impasse. Jonas stood up. The man disgusted him. What kind of scientist was someone who cared only for his own petty gain!

'Think about it. Cash in hand or a worthwhile investment. You've got till tomorrow. After that it's too late.'

Without looking back, Jonas walked to the door and down the stairs. He needed fresh air after the oppressive atmosphere of Paul's flat.

———

F ela walked home by the coast road. She came to a flight of steps that led down to the beach and walked along the strand, taking deep breaths of salt air. Then she began to run, like a dog freed from the leash.

At length she ran out of breath and sat down against a breakwater. She pulled out her mobile phone and called Jonas. He didn't answer, so she left a message, asking him to meet her at Maeve's café in Dún Laoghaire as soon as he could.

The Sunday brunch crowd were leaving and only a few

stragglers remained. Fela was on her third cappuccino and chatting with Maeve when Jonas entered. Seeing him, Maeve got up and returned to the counter. He sat down opposite Fela.

'You're looking positively radiant!'

'It's the sea air. I went for a run.'

'Where have you been since the funeral? I called several times, but your phone was off.'

'Asleep. Then running on the beach.'

'Well, it's done you good.'

Maeve returned with a coffee for Jonas and two slices of Simnel cake. 'I made it myself.'

She set it down before them and returned to the counter. Jonas took a bite of his cake. 'Umm! I'm not surprised you like this place.'

'Maeve's a friend. Her café's one of the main reasons I like living here.'

He took another bite of his cake. 'So what are your plans? I've got nothing on for the rest of the day.'

'We could go into town, catch a movie?'

'D'you have something in mind?'

Her phone rang. She looked at it and stood up. 'Sorry! I need to take this.'

He watched her go over to where the coats were hanging. She had her back to him, and stood cradling the phone to her ear and shifting from foot to foot. After a couple of minutes she returned, looking flushed. 'Sorry about that. A work thing.'

'On Sunday?'

She didn't reply and he said no more. Tears suddenly gathered in her eyes.

'What's it going to be like without Simon?'

'Unimaginable. Will you stay?'

'Where would I go without you two? Estelle called us the Three Musketeers. Now we're down to two!' She paused. 'We came here with such hopes.'

He nodded. 'Real jobs, doing something we believed in...'

'You won the prize.'

'For another man's work. Not much satisfaction in that.'

'You and Simon were always too idealistic. Simon died for it!'

'We don't know that.'

'Whatever happened, he got himself killed and it's an unsolvable mystery. Unless that vaccine shows up one day!'

'And if it did, what would you do?' he asked casually.

'I'd do my best to find out what ruthless, murdering bastard was responsible and see he got what he deserved.'

For a moment he was stifled by conscience. Then he pushed the thought aside. Simon was dead, and nothing could alter that. He smiled at her affectionately.

'If we're going into town, we should make a move.'

———

It was almost ten when Jonas returned to his apartment. He and Fela had gone to an early film, a romantic comedy that left him mildly bored but which she seemed to enjoy. Afterwards they had a pizza and she took the Dart home, while he got the bus to the industrial park.

He poured himself a glass of red and sat down in front of the TV. It was showing a Spaghetti Western he'd seen several times, a landscape of wild hills and dried up canyons that reminded him a little of home. He checked his phone to see if Paul had called but there was no message, not even a missed call. If that was how he wanted it, Jonas would leave him to his fate. He got up, switched off the TV and went to his computer to look up flights to La Paz and Lima.

———

C onrad had called Fela, to make sure she didn't believe their night together had meant nothing to him. But he wasn't overestimating what had happened between them – a young, grief-stricken woman had sought comfort from the nearest she could find to a father substitute. It did, however, complicate their working together. Leaving his feelings aside, if she decided to quit the company that might be best for all of them. He'd do everything he could to help her.

He heard her enter her office, waited a few minutes then opened their communicating door.

'I hope you had a good rest of your weekend,' he said in a tone intended to be affectionate. 'Now we need to gather our forces.'

'Why? Has something happened?'

She switched on her computer without looking at him.

'Weiss wants to talk about the future of R and D. He's off to Switzerland, and that may not turn out too good for the rest of us.'

'You mean our future's at stake?'

'We should be prepared. Have you given any thought to what you might do if they decide to pull out? A year or two in Geneva might not be so bad.'

'Geneva's a bit cosy and provincial for me. I was there once with my mother and I've no wish to go back.'

'It was just a thought. Anyway, if you could give me the details on our new research projects, I'll do my best to talk them up.'

When he'd gone she cursed herself for being so artificial. If she couldn't find a way to be natural with him, she might as well give in her notice now.

———

C onrad knocked at Weiss's door and entered without waiting for an answer. Weiss was on the phone and waved at him to take a seat. He was speaking in German and quickly terminated the conversation. From his expression as he turned to Conrad it was clear he was in a bad mood.

'That was Head Office, as you probably gathered. They're asking what new things we've got in the pipeline. I get the impression they'll only give us until the summer to come up with something solid.'

'We've a young Irish scientist working on a new antibiotic. I'm also looking into research into bioelectronics. That's long term and needs real investment but it has a great future. For the antibiotic we should have preliminary results by the summer.'

'And you see little hope of retrieving the vaccine?'

'I'm afraid Dr Eastlake did a thorough job when he destroyed his research.'

Weiss's face was flushed and his hands on the desk balled into fists.

'We shouldn't give up on it yet. I've managed to track down the scientist who initiated the original research. He's agreed to give us a few weeks of his time. The assistant being off sick doesn't help, so as his manager you'll need to make sure he has whatever he needs and make it a priority.'

He wanted to retort that he was wasting his time, but held his tongue. Weiss obviously knew nothing of the vaccine being offered for sale, though for how long remained to be seen.

'It occurred to me in the meantime we might rebrand the anti-depressant we developed two years ago which sold so well. It's still got plenty of mileage,' said Weiss.

'If you recall, production was halted after a significant number of patients went on to take their own lives. There was a high-profile court case, so we had to withdraw it.'

'You will also recall the case was non-proven. I'd hardly be suggesting this if it hadn't been. Obviously the product would be rebranded and marketed under a different name.'

Disgust overwhelmed Conrad, but he wasn't done yet. He'd contact Estelle's underground connections and do his best to find out who was selling the vaccine, then he'd be gone.

On his way back to his office, he paused in the empty corridor, took out his phone and dialled Estelle's number. She answered at once.

'Hi, it's Conrad. How soon can you set up a meeting with your friends? Okay. I'll wait for your call.'

Half an hour later Estelle called back.

'You've a meeting at nine this evening. It's in a bar down by the old docks just past the bus station. I'll text you the address.'

'Thanks.'

'Don't balls it up! It's my reputation on the line as well as yours.'

She rang off. He had no idea if he'd be meeting one person or several, or what they might ask for in return. He'd just have to keep his wits about him.

———

The bar had a low stucco ceiling stained by tobacco smoke, and a flagged floor unevenly worn by years of seamen's boots. Gentrification had not yet caught up with this part of town, and there was only a handful of regulars, silent or engaged in the muttered monologues of lonely men. Conrad ordered a Guinness and tried to avoid the attention of his neighbour, seated unsteadily on a barstool. As soon as his drink was ready, he carried it over to an empty booth and sat down to wait.

A few minutes later Estelle entered the bar, followed by a short, stocky young woman of around thirty wearing a flak jacket and combat boots. Estelle gestured the woman in his direction and went over to the bar.

'Hi! I'm Charlie,' she said, as she sat down. 'You must be Conrad Dreyer.'

Her voice was pleasantly low and melodious.

'Yes. Thanks for coming.'

'It's not a social visit.'

'I realise that.'

He caught the laughter in her gaze and began to relax.

Estelle returned with two glasses of Jameson's and placed one in front of Charlie.

'So you've introduced yourselves. I've told Charlie about Simon, but perhaps you should tell her yourself what you want from her.'

Conrad nodded. He'd thought there'd be more preliminaries but clearly not.

'Dr Eastlake destroyed his vaccine because he believed it had dangerous side effects and innocent people were going to be experimented on. A practice, as you know, many companies are all too ready to engage in. Now it appears someone has got hold of the formula and is once again offering the drug for sale. I need to find out who that is, and put a stop to it.'

'And what's in this for you?'

'You could say it's a matter of principle.'

Charlie looked at him with a quizzical expression. 'Very noble!'

'You may not believe an employee of a pharma company can have principles, but it happens. I'm not an idealist, but I won't be party to fraudulent dealings. Especially when someone's died for his beliefs.'

'So you want us to find out who's involved?'

'And most importantly put a stop to them.'

'And if we succeed and you get back the formula, what guarantee do we have you'll destroy it and not use it for your own gain? Big money can be seductive, even for those who are convinced of their own incorruptibility.'

'You can witness its destruction. As for whether or not that's truly the end of it, I guess you just have to accept my word.'

Charlie regarded him as she emptied her glass then got up from the bench. 'We'll get back to you in a few days.'

'A few days will be too late. The stuff's already out there. A deal could be finalised any minute.'

'We know how these things work. Just don't do anything till you hear from us.' She reached out her hand. 'Goodbye, Dr Dreyer. It's good to meet an "honest" pharma man!'

He watched her determined, stocky figure walk to the door and disappear onto the street.

'So we just wait to see what happens?' he said to Estelle. 'Anyway, thanks for setting up the meeting. I liked her.'

'You surprise me!'

'Not quite the bigot you thought me!'

She laughed. 'You don't fool me, Conrad Dreyer!'

———

Jonas locked up his lab at the end of a long day. He was working on the crops most likely to give the best yields as a result of genetic modification. It wasn't an area the company had been involved in before, but Weiss was eager to find out if it was worthy of investment, and Jonas needed to keep up appearances for a little longer.

Most people had gone home and he wanted to follow

suit, pour himself a drink, put his feet up and listen to some music. But he had something urgent to do. The Guatemalans required authorisation from someone senior before they'd agree to finalise the vaccine deal, and that had to be Weiss. He'd find a pretext to get the keys from the night manager and search Weiss's office. With luck, still hoping for a deal, he'd have hung onto the documents. It was even possible he'd already signed them, believing the sale to be imminent. If not, his signature shouldn't be too hard to forge.

His mobile rang. It was Paul. 'Listen, you bastard, how much are you offering?'

'You've changed your mind!'

'That depends. How much?'

'A fifth of what I get.'

'You must be bloody joking! I saved those copies. It's my work. Half!'

'There'll be no deal at all if I can't get a legitimate sale. I'll be in touch.'

'You better had. This isn't the last you'll hear from me.'

'I'll call you.'

Paul could do nothing on his own. He'd find out soon enough that greed meant he'd get nothing.

———

Conrad tossed and turned. A faint trace of Fela's scent on the pillow tormented him. Details of her face, mouth and body surfaced and resurfaced. Eventually he got up, went into the living room and poured himself a whisky. Through the window the moon gave the ripples on the water a golden sheen, like shifting desert sands. He thought of Djibouti where he'd waited out his last mission with his fellow Legionnaires, polishing their weapons and carrying out stupid endurance tests to pass the time. It was the camaraderie he missed, not the action. They were supposed to save lives, but in truth their interventions mostly served the interests of someone else's politics or profit. He took a sip of whisky, stretched out on the sofa and closed his eyes.

In the morning he woke late after a fitful sleep, got up, took a quick shower, and drove to the office. Fela was already bent over her computer screen, filled with columns of figures. In a spontaneous gesture he reached out to stroke her unruly hair, feeling its silky texture between his fingers. She caught his hand in hers and held it for a moment, without turning to look at him. Then she replaced her hand on the keyboard and pressed print. She handed him a page of figures with a smile that made his heart miss a beat. He thanked her and returned to his room.

His phone rang.

'Dr Dreyer? It's Charlie.'

'Charlie! Any news?'

'Yes, but not good, I'm afraid. The vaccine has been sold.'

Shock silenced him.

'Are you still there?'

'Yes. Sorry!'

'Our contact confirms the Guatemalan embassy took delivery first thing this morning.'

'Who from? Do you have a name?'

'All we know is that the deal was done in the name of your company, Associated Swiss Pharmaceuticals.'

Conrad swallowed.

'Dr Dreyer?'

'Yes. If you find out anything more, any names, please call me.'

'Okay, though you may be best placed to find out more. You're an insider.' Charlie rang off.

If Weiss were responsible, he would surely have seen signs. It was possible someone more senior from HQ had intervened, though the speed of the deal made that unlikely. He needed to talk to Estelle.

He left the office and went down to the canteen to call her. The canteen was empty and he sat down at a table in the far corner. She answered at once.

'I know,' she said, recognising his voice. 'I guess it's over. Too late to stop them now.'

'I have to find out who authorised this. And how they got hold of the formula.'

He kept his voice low.

'Good luck!'

'Is that all?'

'I've got a tutorial in five minutes. I'll call you this afternoon. Till then, do nothing. I know how rash you can be.'

'I'll come to the university.'

'Not before three. I'm teaching.'

He pocketed his phone. He needed to think.

F ela printed out the rest of the figures Conrad had asked for and kept an ear out for his return. The way he'd laid his hand on her hair that morning made her think he wasn't distancing himself from her, and the world took back some of its colour.

By late morning he still hadn't returned, but calling him seemed intrusive. She decided to take an early lunch and walk into the village for a sandwich. As she came out of the deli, her gaze drifted across the square and her eye was caught by someone who looked remarkably like Conrad, walking along the far side of it. As she watched he approached a telephone box, one of two that had been installed in a nostalgic gesture towards the tiny handful of people without mobiles, or those who required anonymity. He entered, spoke briefly into the receiver then hung up. The bus to the airport was pulling up at the far end of the square, where several people with suitcases were already waiting. She observed him leave the box, hurry towards the bus and board it. A moment later the bus drove off.

She sat down on a nearby bench to eat her sandwich. He'd said nothing about being out for the day, and she could think of no reason why he'd be going to the airport.

Back in her office, she spent the rest of the afternoon trying to concentrate and listening for his return. It took her back to childhood hours spent waiting – for her friend to call, or for her mother to get dressed, to come home from work or a night out with friends. Perhaps that was why she'd always felt driven by the need to be punctual. Unlike Simon, who'd never been on time and sometimes failed to show up altogether. In the end she could endure it no longer and called Jonas to join her in the canteen for a coffee. The call went to answerphone but he'd no doubt call back in a few minutes.

———

C onrad sat on the airport bus, rereading the text Charlie had sent him following their brief phone call. It read, 'Unidentified male seen entering Shelbourne Hotel 10 last night. Met with man known to be agent of Guatemalan government staying at hotel. First man handed over package and received large envelope. Left a few minutes later.'

It was already after two. With luck he'd be at the airport in time to intercept the embassy official waiting to board the flight to Guatemala City. As soon as he arrived, he'd get a message put out over the tannoy that Dr Weiss urgently needed to speak to him before embarkation.

The traffic was bad as usual and the bus was delayed. He ran to the departures area. The man might already have gone through, in which case he'd have to get authorisation to meet him on the other side, which would take time. He had the name and some idea of what he looked like from the photo Charlie had forwarded to his phone, though the image was blurred and not easy to make out. His best chance was to check the airline's passenger list and put out an urgent call.

He waited impatiently as the person in front in the queue talked interminably to the attendant behind the counter. As he glanced restlessly around, he suddenly caught sight of a familiar figure standing at the KLM counter across the hall. With a shock, he realised it was Jonas. He was carrying a backpack and as Conrad watched, the official handed him a ticket and he set off in the direction of departures.

At that moment the man in front of him concluded his business, and the attendant called for his attention. He couldn't leave without asking about the Guatemalan, but by then he'd have lost Jonas. It was too late for messages, the attendant said, since the plane was already on the runway. Losing no more time, Conrad thanked him and hurried off towards the departure gates.

He stood at the barrier, scanning the lines of people waiting to pass through baggage control. At length he spotted Jonas in the third queue. He was taking off his jacket and shoes and placing them in a plastic tray next to another that contained his backpack. As Conrad watched, he was called to the electronic gate and the luggage belt moved on. In seconds he had passed through without a hitch, and was lost to sight.

Conrad stood rooted to the spot, unable to decide what to do next. Where was Jonas going and why without a word to anyone, not even Fela? Then he remembered Charlie's text about the unknown man going to The Shelbourne to meet the Guatemalan. Could that man have been Jonas? If so, incredible as it seemed, he should go to airport police directly and get him brought back for questioning. But on what grounds? And even if he persuaded the police to cooperate, the vaccine was already sold and on its way out of the country. He was too late.

He took the bus back to town, his mind in turmoil. If only he'd got on to Charlie sooner, he might have been in time to intercept the Guatemalan. He'd tried, but she wasn't picking up her phone. Still it was his fault for being too slow off the mark. And then there was the mystery of Jonas.

Estelle had said to come after three and it wasn't quite four. He'd rather not go at all, but he needed to talk to her about what he'd seen. The security guard knew him by sight, and let him into the campus. She was on the second floor of one of the newer blocks, overlooking a pool with fountains. He climbed the stairs and knocked.

'Come in!'

He entered, closing the door behind him. A large window facing southwest admitted light off the water that lit up the room on even this greyest of days.

'Coffee?' she said. 'Or by the look of you, maybe something stronger.'

She took a bottle of Paddy's and a glass from a drawer in her desk. He shook his head and sat down opposite her. 'You've heard?'

'About the vaccine?'

She nodded. 'Charlie called.'

'She sent me a text and I went to the airport to try and intercept the guy from Guatemala.'

'And?'

'I was too late. But I saw someone else.'

She looked at him expectantly.

'Jonas.'

'Jonas! What was he doing there?'

'He bought a ticket from KLM, which suggests it was a long-haul flight. I've a suspicion he was the man seen with the Guatemalan in the Shelbourne last night.'

'Have you any evidence?'

Conrad shook his head and ran a hand through his thick chestnut hair, peppered now with grey.

'But why else would he be boarding a plane with no warning or word to anyone?'

'How could he have got hold of the formula?'

'I don't know. But the thought of that stuff being sold and the harm it may do to innocent kids makes me sick. Jonas of all people, a liar and a thief!'

'Don't damn him till we have proof. The airport will have a record of his destination.'

'I should have waited to check. All I could think of was getting away from there.'

'If it is Jonas, he couldn't have pulled off this deal by himself.'

'I'm pretty sure Weiss knows nothing.'

'So who authorised it?'

'That's what I need to find out.'

He stood up. 'I'd better be going. Let me know if you hear anything more.'

'Of course.'

It was after six when Conrad got back to his office. Fela had already gone and left no message. It wasn't good, leaving her all day without a word, but it couldn't be helped. The simplest thing was to tell her about the sale of the vaccine, which would explain everything. But the situation was too confused, and the possibility of Jonas being involved would be another blow.

———

Fela reached home and parked her bike in front of the house. She sat down on the front steps in the warm evening sunshine and took her phone out of her pocket to call Jonas. His lab had been empty when she dropped by and she hadn't heard from him for over twenty-four hours. After a few rings it went to answer phone. She decided not to leave another message and to try again in a little while.

She walked along the quayside as far as the café. She could see Maeve through the window, busy laying tables. It looked as though she was expecting a crowd in, so Fela carried on walking. A breeze was blowing up and the metal hawsers of sailing boats made strange music as the crafts rose and fell with the swell. In the distance the ferry from Holyhead was edging its way into port, to disgorge another flood of cars and people upon the town.

Her thoughts turned to Conrad. She hardly dared ask herself what she hoped for from the relationship, if it could be called that. In the end it was only Jonas who kept her here. There was a ping from the phone in her pocket as it received a message. She pulled it out and gazed at the screen. The message appeared to have been sent a couple of hours ago and read, 'Shan't be around this evening. But check your email tomorrow. Love you, Jonas.' It was unlike Jonas to be so mysterious, and now she'd have to wait until morning. Meanwhile there was the evening to get through. She turned back in the direction of Maeve's café.

————

Jonas settled down for the long flight to Lima. His mind was too distracted to read or take in a movie. Burning his boats was a desperate measure, but he'd made his choice. Part of the money he had with him. The bulk was waiting in a bank in Lima in the company's name, for which he alone had the passcode. He would use it to set up his research project, the realisation of a lifetime's dream.

Of all his regrets the chief was Fela, though even that wasn't enough to overcome his feelings of excitement. If he'd had a choice, he'd have explained his reasons face to face, done his best to make her understand. But that would have been too risky, and besides there wasn't time. If he succeeded, he would make her proud, and in the end she might forgive him.

He pulled out his laptop. Writing an email to her was one of the hardest things he'd ever done. Still grieving for Simon and her father, he knew the blow it would be to be left alone, the last musketeer. If there'd been any chance she could have loved him as more than a friend, he might have begged her to come with him. Fela was the only woman he'd ever felt seriously drawn to, possibly because he'd always known she wasn't available. He wasn't made for intimacy, or perhaps it was just too risky. Either way it scarcely mattered, since all his energies must now be concentrated on the future. Still he wanted his leave-taking of her to be as honest as possible.

'Dear Fela,' he wrote.

When you get this, I'll be gone. I wish I could have

spoken to you face to face but that was impossible. By the time I learned what was going on, the vaccine had already been offered for sale. I recognise that in the end, as I'm the one to benefit, I'm also a thief, and I accept that guilt. But unlike the original thief, I'm not driven by greed, but rather by the ambition to bring something worthwhile out of the awful tragedy of Simon's death. If my plan succeeds, it will benefit not just sick people all over the world, but also those desperate tribes on the edge of extinction who inhabit the wild places where I'll be working. My aim is to use the money to build a team to develop medicines based on traditional plant remedies, especially in the field of antibiotics, medicines that will be effective with virtually no side effects.

This may sound absurdly grandiose, but over the years I've been gathering research and I believe with the right helpers we can make it work. It's the direction we as a civilisation must take – even eventually the big pharmaceuticals, as Simon agreed. Perhaps, if I'm successful, it will go some way towards redeeming the awful pointlessness of his death.

The hardest thing is leaving you, the last of we 'three musketeers'. If I'd thought you might come with me, I'd have begged you on my knees. But I have no such illusions. I see no future for either of us in this company and hope with all my heart you too will find a better and more satisfying way to live.

You may say the end can never justify the means. But I would disagree. Whether I succeed or fail, it's quite likely you won't ever want to hear from me again. But if the project gets off the ground, I will try to contact you.

So wish me luck. Forgive me if you can for not being a better friend to you. Believe me, it isn't for lack of love. Perhaps next time we meet there'll be something to celebrate and the world will feel a brighter place.

Jonas

He read the email again then pressed send. It wouldn't go until they touched down in Atlanta before the next leg to Lima, but she should get it in the morning.

———

F ela woke late with a hangover. She'd ended up staying at Maeve's until after closing, and she wasn't used to drinking too much. She tried to remember what they'd talked about, and thought it was love. She recalled telling Maeve about her night with Conrad, and that however much she tried it was impossible to go back to how things were before. She even admitted her jealousy of Estelle. Maeve listened, but whatever wise words she'd offered were forgotten by morning. Still, as Maeve said, trouble shared was trouble halved.

She rode to the company building, left her bike in the car park, and went up to her office. The prospect of seeing Conrad brought an unbidden flicker of excitement. But as she entered her office, she saw their communicating door was closed. He too must be late, and she refused to specu-late on how he'd spent the evening. She hung up her coat, changed her boots for shoes, and opened up her computer.

There was an email from Conrad, saying he wouldn't be in till ten and to take things easy until then. She'd missed breakfast so decided to go down to the canteen. As she waited for the lift at the end of the corridor, her mobile pinged with the receipt of another email. She ignored it and entered the lift.

In the canteen she took her tray over to an empty table and sat down with her favourite smoked salmon bagel and coffee. As she ate, she remembered Jonas's message the night before telling her to expect an email in the morning that would explain everything. She opened her phone. The message was from him, a long one, so she decided to finish her breakfast before reading it.

She left the canteen through the side door, walked to the low wall that surrounded the car park, sat down and pulled out her phone. She read the message quickly then read it over again. Incredulity forced her to concentrate as one astonishing word piled on top of another. Jonas had gone, taking with him Simon's formula. The vaccine, like a curse, had destroyed first one then the other, because if Jonas wasn't actually dead he might as well have been. Even if his crazy scheme worked out, he'd be viewed as a criminal and could never return. In all the years they'd known each other, she'd failed to see what desperate ambition drove him. But worst of all, how had he got hold of the formula?

She barely noticed as Conrad's Jeep entered the car park. He got out, came towards her and sat down beside her on the wall. Neither spoke. In the silence he breathed in the heady scent of lime blossom that drifted down from the trees above.

'Has something happened?' he asked at length.

She looked up and passed him her phone.

'I just got this.'

He read the email carefully.

'I thought Simon was the maverick,' he said, meeting her gaze.

'How did he get hold of the formula?'

'That indeed is the question.'

'Maybe he was the one who followed Simon.' Her voice was little more than a whisper.

'I don't believe he's capable of that.'

'But how can we be sure?'

He stood up. 'Give me a few minutes. We can take the Jeep and get out of here.'

Waiting for his return, she reread Jonas's email for the third time. Simon and now Jonas, the people she thought she knew best, had committed actions she could never have imagined possible. Perhaps she'd invented images of people who'd never existed. Or perhaps no one, herself included, could be sure of what they might do if circumstances arose.

———

For several miles they drove in silence. Fela felt weightless as though at any moment she might melt into air. The anchors that had grounded her for almost ten years had been hauled up, and she was adrift. She scarcely noticed when Conrad turned off the motorway and headed for the hills.

The day was fresh and fair, and as they climbed higher she wound down her window and breathed in scents of wild herbs and rank traces of sheep. Above them a flock of honking geese flew in formation across a sky mottled with cloud. They reached a plateau scattered with rocks and heather and Conrad pulled off the road. There was no sound, except the mewing cry of a buzzard and bees combing the wildflowers. Far below was a lake. White birds swam on its surface and beside it stood a small hut.

He took a rucksack from the back of the Jeep and opened her passenger door.

'Come on! It's not far.'

'Where are we going?'

He pointed to the hut beside the lake. 'Sometimes I stay there. We can boil a kettle and have something to eat.'

'I'm not hungry.'

'A drink then? It's nice to sit by the lake.'

She followed him down the hill via a steep path. Once or twice she stumbled, and he reached out to steady her but quickly let her go.

When they reached the hut, he found the key under a stone, unlocked it and brought out a folding chair, which he placed for her at the edge of the water. A few minutes later he emerged from the hut with two mugs of tea. He handed her one and sat down on a rock a short distance away. Neither of them spoke, but she felt comforted by his presence.

Eventually the sun disappeared behind the mountain and it grew chilly. Inside the hut Conrad made a fire, lit the oil lamp and cobbled together a meal from some tins in the store cupboard and the few provisions he'd brought with him in his rucksack. He produced a bottle of whisky, adding water from the kettle and a lump of sugar to make hot toddies. Whatever he offered she accepted with scarcely a word, content just to be in his company.

'Do want to go back or stay the night?' he asked, when they had eaten.

'I never want to go back!' she replied in a low voice.

'We can sleep here then.'

She nodded.

He unrolled a mattress from its plastic cover then produced a sleeping bag from his rucksack, which he laid out on the mattress. In the cupboard he found two blankets, one for her and one for himself in the chair. When the bed was ready he invited her to lie down. She took off her boots and jeans and got into the sleeping bag. He rolled a cigarette, poured himself another whisky and settled into the chair. He could hear from her breathing that she'd fallen asleep almost at once, but it was still not fully dark and he wasn't ready for sleep. He threw another log on the fire, and went out to smoke under the stars.

When he returned, she was awake and said softly, 'Aren't you coming to bed?'

'You want me to?'

She held open the sleeping bag.

He took off his outer clothes and got in beside her, lying as still as he could not to betray his desire. It was comfort she needed, not sex. She moved against him.

'Love is the best comfort,' she whispered, as if reading his thoughts.

He drew her closer, placing a hand on her belly. She let it rest there for a moment, then slid it down over her navel towards her pubis. He kissed her warm neck under the mane of hair, and let his hand slide between her legs as she tilted her face to his, seeking his kiss. She tasted the whisky and trace of tobacco on his breath as he entered her. Such pure pleasure, healing in its very impersonality, filled the darkness inside her with its warmth.

In the morning Conrad made coffee and they ate the last of the bread and cheese out by the lake. She noted how deftly he carried out each task, providing whatever was needed without fuss. The morning was overcast but mild, and she decided to take a swim before leaving. As she entered the water, the cold took her breath away and she plunged quickly under the surface. A dozen strokes and she was out again, shivering but triumphant.

'Aren't you going in?'

'I'm happy to watch you.'

'You have to go in too!'

Reluctantly he took off his clothes and waded in until, unable to endure such slow torture, he dived, swam a few metres with a swift crawl and headed back to shore. When he emerged, his limbs glowed pink and he shook his wet head like a dog, then took off at speed along the water's edge. She laughed to see him and held out a towel to wrap him in when he returned.

Inside the hut he built up the fire again, while she made tea. They put on sweaters and, as they sipped the tea, agreed that swimming in the fresh water of a mountain lake beat sea bathing every time.

'I'd like to stay here forever!' She squatted down beside the fire.

'There's enough fish in the lake. And if we got sick of fish I guess I could catch a hare.'

'Splendid!'

He was silent for a moment, then said, 'I wish it were that easy.'

'You mean we have to go.'

'I'm afraid so.'

The joy left her face. Reaching for the whisky bottle, he poured a shot into his cup and offered it to her. She shook her head.

'Drinking in the day makes me depressed.'

He drank down the last of his tea, gathered up his belongings and stuffed them into his rucksack. She searched around for her boots and put them on. Apart from her jacket, there was nothing else she'd brought with her. He locked the door and together they climbed the steep path to where they'd left the Jeep. At the top she turned and looked back at the lake below.

She knew she would always remember this place.

As they drove back, her thoughts returned to the vaccine. 'D'you think Weiss knows yet?'

'I doubt it. Unless Jonas wrote to him too!'

'But how could he have pulled it off on his own?'

'I ask myself that. Maybe he got hold of the original sale agreement.'

'But wouldn't that have to go through Weiss?'

'Everything was agreed. All it needed was a final signature.'

'And he could have forged that?'

'Easily, I think.'

She paused. 'We still don't know how he got hold of the formula.'

'That's the tough one.'

At midday Conrad went to Weiss for his daily briefing. Sometimes this took over an hour. Today it took barely ten minutes. Weiss talked about the arrival of Dr Murphy, the previous researcher, due to take place later that day. He was agitated, but it was clear he knew nothing about the sale. On his way back to his office, Conrad dropped by Simon's old lab. It was locked, so he called Maloney and asked him to come up with the keys.

As he waited for him in the corridor, he wondered why the lab assistant wasn't back at work. Then he remembered he was off sick. Maloney appeared, unlocked the door and handed him the keys. Inside he went through the desks and filing cabinets in case something might have been missed, but found nothing significant. Codes for all the computers were held on a central register, and Weiss kept those relating to R and D. Molly, his secretary, could no doubt give him what he needed if he asked her.

He got the codes and returned to the lab. A new hard drive had been installed to replace the one removed by Simon, but it was empty. Paul's was also blank. His claim to have started work on retrieving the formula had obviously been a pretence. He sat at Paul's desk, trying to think. Could Jonas have wiped the CCTV footage Fela had found missing on the night of Simon's death? The idea of him murdering his best friend was unthinkable, yet how else would he have known Simon had his hard drives with him? And if it wasn't him, how had he got hold of the formula? Weiss might have been involved, but he didn't even know the vaccine had been sold. None of it made sense.

One thing he could check was whether the original sale document for the vaccine was still in Weiss' office or had gone missing. He knew where he kept the keys to his filing cabinets. If he waited till his secretary had gone home, he could make a search. He wasn't sure if the office was individually alarmed, but Maloney could tell him. He left the lab, locking the door behind him.

———

A t five thirty, after a day spent with the routine tasks of accounting, Fela closed down her computer. She'd hoped Conrad would call or make a belated appearance, but in the end she left a note on his desk, saying she was leaving for the day. It was no use pretending indifference. He was all she could think of, despite doing her best to persuade herself that sex between adults who liked each other was no big deal.

On her way home she took a shortcut through the backstreets of Blackrock. She pulled up at a traffic light and her attention was drawn to a lively group of people who'd spilled onto the pavement outside a bar. She was in no hurry to get back to the solitude of her flat and decided to stop for a quick drink. She left her bike in the neighbouring side street and threaded her way through the revellers.

Inside, the place was half empty, except for the usual drunks propping up the bar and a handful of young men gathered around a pool table. She turned to go and was halfway out of the door, when someone seized her by the arm and a slightly slurred voice said,

'Where are you rushing off to?'

She recognised his face but, unshaven and rather dishevelled, she couldn't at first place him. He supported himself on a crutch and one leg of his jeans had been slit from ankle to knee to accommodate a cast. She shook her arm free.

'Felicity O'Connor! It's Paul!'

'Paul! Sorry, I wasn't sure.' Her manner softened a little. He was obviously taking Simon's death hard.

'What happened to you?' She indicated his leg in plaster.

'You haven't heard? Ask your friend Jonas, Dr Finzi.'

He grinned unpleasantly, and she felt an urgent need to escape.

'Let's have coffee sometime. In the canteen.'

'I'm off sick.'

'When you're back then. I hope that won't be too long.'

'If you want to talk, I'll be at my flat, 154 Manor St, Stoneybatter. There's things about Dr Finzi you might like to know.'

Her throat constricted. Was there more Jonas hadn't told her?

'Okay. I'll be in touch.'

With a deft sidestep she walked past him and found herself once more out on the street.

Riding back to her house, she thought about Paul's invitation. Visiting him was the last thing she wanted, but if he knew something about Jonas she needed to find out.

She wondered whether to tell Conrad of the encounter, but instinct warned her not to involve him yet.

————

Conrad let himself into Weiss's office with the key he'd borrowed from Maloney. Weiss had left earlier for town with an executive from HQ, and Maloney said his office was only alarmed after he made his final evening rounds. Conrad found Weiss's private keys in a compartment on the underside of his desk where he'd seen him stow them, and began systematically searching the drawers. Finding nothing of interest, he moved on to the filing cabinet. There was a file labelled 'Vaccine' but no sign of a sale agreement, just a printed email from a representative from Guatemala with time and place for a meeting. If an agreement existed, and he felt sure it had, it had been removed. Jonas had either forged a signature, or the documents had already been signed in preparation for an imminent deal. He'd probably never know for sure, and Jonas would shortly be buried too deep in the Amazon jungle for extradition. He replaced the keys in their hiding place and left the office, locking the door behind him.

Walking back down the corridor he took out his phone and called Estelle.

————

Fela's sleep was full of dreams. In the morning she felt as though she'd hardly slept a wink, recalling little but the feeling of menace. She dressed in her dowdiest clothes and made a strong coffee, before setting off for Stoneybatter.

She pressed the bell at the side entrance to Paul's flat and waited. When it wasn't answered she pressed again. After a few more seconds Paul's voice answered, 'Yes?'

'It's Fela, your colleague from work. Can I come up?'

There was a brief pause. 'Top of the stairs.'

The buzzer went and she entered a narrow hallway that smelt of cooking fat and stale cigarette smoke. When she reached the top, she saw his front door was ajar. She tapped and went in.

The living room was off a small passage. Paul was sitting in an armchair, his injured leg propped up on a stool. The room was airless and littered with pizza boxes, old beer cans, and an overflowing ashtray. A chewed dog basket with a filthy blanket lay in one corner, but there was no sign of a dog.

'My sister's visiting friends, with the dog,' Paul said, following her gaze. 'If I'd known you were coming I'd have tidied up.'

'Could we open a window?'

'Help yourself.'

She had to push hard at the metal casement, as if it hadn't been opened in years.

'You said you had something to tell me about Dr Finzi,' she said, perching on the edge of the sofa.

'When it gets out he's sold the vaccine it'll cause a real stink!' Paul chuckled.

His remark shocked her. She could scarcely believe Jonas had confided in Paul, yet how else would he know?

Paul got up from his chair and limped over to the small

kitchen off the living room. She heard the fridge open and close and he called out, 'Want a beer?'

'No thanks.'

He returned, sat down and cracked one open. 'Yes, I'm afraid your friend Dr Finzi's a thief.' He took a swig.

'How did he get hold of the formula?'

'Ah, that's the question! I have my ideas, but I need to talk to the garda first, don't you think?'

She did her best not to rise to his provocation.

'You think Jonas stole it from Dr Eastlake?'

'Could be.'

She forced herself to keep calm. 'It's Simon, Dr Eastlake, who's the wronged party in all this. For his sake, if Jonas took the hard drive from him it must be made known.'

'Why should I tell you anything?'

'Both of them are my friends. I need to know if Jonas followed Simon to the mountains.'

He shrugged. 'I can't tell you that. All I know is he offered to pay for my silence when I found out what he was up to. I'm no saint. I agreed.'

'And did he?'

He shook his head. 'Scarpered without handing over a penny. More fool me for trusting him!'

'I'm sorry for that. But how did he get hold of it?'

'Sorry! I can't help you there.'

She didn't trust Paul. Yet it was clear he and Jonas had had some sort of agreement, something else she found almost impossible to believe.

'Are you going to tell Weiss what you know?'

'You think I'd be believed? They'd blame it all on me.'

'Why should they?'

'They want a scapegoat for losing the vaccine. Someone to throw the book at.'

'That's just paranoid. All they want is the truth.'

He laughed. 'You think Weiss doesn't need someone to blame for his own stupidity? How, for example, did Dr Finzi get hold of the sale documents, since he'd hardly manage to flog the stuff off in his own name?'

He was right, of course. She felt sick at heart.

'When it comes down to it, Weiss is just as responsible, and his bosses will want to know how he let it happen.'

Revulsion for this grotty room, with its stench of wet dog, beer, and fag ends, was starting to overwhelm her.

'He's not what you think, your Dr Finzi.' He gestured at his injured leg. 'Want to know how I got this?'

'No doubt you'll tell me.' Things, she realised, were about to get worse.

'He shoved me down the stairs next to the labs.'

'You mean you fell.'

'I know what I fucking mean! It was no accident. He'd have done for me properly if he could. Unlucky for him I'm still here.'

'Why on earth would he have wanted to do that?'

'Because I had what he wanted!'

She tensed, scenting a confession. 'You were the one who had the foresight to copy the formula, and he stole it from you?'

His eyes glinted with malice. 'He might call himself chief scientist, but he wasn't as smart as he thought. He understood nothing of our work, and I knew Simon was about to destroy everything we'd done. My work as much as his!'

Pride at his own cleverness, mingled with his sense of injustice, had overcome his instinct for self-preservation.

'You outwitted them all, only to be cheated by Dr Finzi!'

He nodded.

'And a broken ankle as payment! I understand your anger!' she said, picking up her bag.

'I have to go. I hope your leg's better soon. I'll let you know what happens when the news is out.'

He shrugged. 'It makes little difference to me now. I'm done with the lot of them.'

She almost ran down the stairs, and when she reached the street kept on running. Eventually she came to a churchyard and sank down on a bench amongst the gravestones to get her breath. The morning was overcast with a light drizzle, but her surroundings scarcely registered. It was clear now. Paul had copied the hard drive and Jonas, her friend, had pushed Paul down the stairs in order to steal the copy. In the process Paul had broken his ankle and Jonas had left without paying a penny of what he'd promised. She thought of Jonas's email telling of his lofty plans and deep affection. She felt as though she were in a hall of mirrors where every reflection distorted and nothing was what it seemed. Not even the noblest of intentions could justify such dirty actions. She got up and left the graveyard.

———

W hen she entered the company building, she was at once aware of the tension. The receptionist broke off her phone call and greeted her in a distracted manner, and on her way up to her office she passed a couple of researchers engaged in urgent conversation, who fell silent as she passed. When she reached her office the communicating door was open and Conrad was standing in the middle of the room.

'They know?' she asked, taking off her boots and hanging up her jacket.

'It appears so.'

'When did this happen?'

'Weiss heard this morning. He's in a towering rage. Wild accusations are flying everywhere. He told me he suspected Simon of intending to sell the stuff all along to some third party but the deal went wrong. That's why he was killed.'

'That's insane!'

'He's talking of hiring private detectives.'

'Does he know about Jonas?'

'Jonas hasn't been mentioned. The story is he's off sick.'

'So what do we do now?'

'Wait, and in the meantime do our best to find out if it was him who took the hard drives.'

'Best leave it to the private eyes!'

It took him a moment to catch her irony. 'Agh!... I talked to some people last night who verified Jonas had made contact with the Guatemalans.'

'What people?'

'People who monitor pharma companies to expose their dirty dealings.'

'You're keeping company with eco warriors now?'

'They can be useful.'

She paused. Conrad wasn't the one who deserved her anger. 'I can do better than any private eye.'

He looked at her questioningly.

'This morning I went to visit Simon's assistant Paul. I ran into him at a bar the previous night and it was clear he had something he needed to get off his chest.'

He waited for her to continue.

'He knew Simon intended to destroy his hard drives so he copied them. Jonas found out and stole them from him.'

She refrained from saying how Jonas had pushed Paul down the stairs and nearly killed him.

Conrad digested this in silence.

'The only question that remains is whether someone followed Simon to the Wicklow mountains.'

'Perhaps the Garda are right after all,' he said. 'It was just an accident.'

'I don't believe it. I've accepted my father's death may never be resolved. I'm not going to let Simon's remain a mystery. '

He thought of Estelle's words, 'You're swimming in the shark pool now!' and placed his hand on her shoulder.

'Let's get through today then sleep on it. Tomorrow we'll try to make better sense of things.'

The evening was fine and warm. Fela drove to her favourite spot down the coast and took a long walk along the strand. The sea, with its restless motion and ever-changing colours, never failed to calm her. When she returned home and drew up outside her house, she saw Conrad waiting across the street. He was leaning against the wall, smoking one of his dark tobacco roll-ups. She locked her helmet into its space beneath the seat and crossed the road to meet him.

He smiled and stubbed out his cigarette as she approached. 'You look refreshed.'

'I took a walk. That always helps.'

'Can I come in for a minute? I brought you this.' He produced a packet of herbal tea and offered it to her.

'It's supposed to be calming and invigorating. A friend gets it at the market and swears by it for all ailments.'

The packet was plain except for a few handwritten words. The friend, she assumed, was Estelle.

'If it's invigorating I'd rather leave it till morning. But I've got wine.'

She unlocked the door and led the way upstairs, stepping quietly so as not to disturb her landlords. Inside the flat she dumped her bag and jacket on the nearest chair and went to the kitchen.

'Mind if I make a tea?' Conrad said, following her.

'Why not? I'll have a sip of yours to see the effect.'

She gestured towards the kettle and placed a mug and two glasses from the cupboard on the table.

When the kettle boiled he put a pinch of herbs into the

mug, filled it with hot water and pushed it towards her. 'It needs to brew for a few minutes.'

She sniffed it. 'It smells like the southern maquis!'

He nodded. 'It smells of Corsica.'

She leaned back in her chair. 'Tell me about Corsica.'

'What d'you want to know?'

'About you, a young man in the Foreign Legion.'

He paused for a moment, as if trying to recollect. 'I was in the Second Foreign Parachute Regiment, based at Camp Raffalli near Calvi. The island is very rocky and the mountains come down to the sea. In summer the sea can go quickly from calm to crashing wild. The hot wind from the mountains meets the cool air from the sea and stirs up the waves. There are birds of prey, kites and buzzards, lots of them, and in winter it can be very cold.'

She folded her hands in front of her, captured by his words.

'The island has its own smell. When you arrive the first thing you smell is the curry plant, and in the maquis your footsteps crushing the herbs and wild plants give off a rare, delicious scent.

'The Corsicans have a saying that nothing good ever came from the sea, so the villages are built inland, with narrow cobbled streets and stones the colour of the hills they cling to. At first sight they're invisible.'

'So where did you land your parachutes?'

'The camp was on the coast, so the planes flew out over the sea, turned and dropped us on their way back. We'd do ten or twelve jumps a day when preparing for a mission, as well as running miles with heavy backpacks in the heat of the day. We needed to be fit.'

'Life must have been hard!'

'Not if you did what you had to and obeyed the rules. Like most highly trained animals, we got pleasure out of carrying out the tasks we learned. Life was simple, and for me like most of the others that was a relief. There was a sense of camaraderie, a feeling of mutual trust. Most of us young recruits had never known that.'

She did her best to picture what it must have been like on that remote island, struggling with a language you barely understood and a bunch of rough strangers, to sink or swim.

'Do you miss it?'

'The landscape maybe – running at evening or in the early morning in that amazing light. And the silence, except for the occasional bird and the wind in the euca-lyptus trees. There were days like that too in Africa, some remote corner where the only relief from the sun was a rock or a wizened tree. Then suddenly you came across a creek, narrow and deep enough to keep the water fresh and cool, and you plunged in.'

'Would you ever go back?'

'Those were the good bits. And anyway you can't go back, even if you want to, and I don't.'

He offered her the mug. She took a sip and returned it to him. 'It's good!'

He nodded and they shared the rest of the tea. At length he stood up. 'I'd better go. I just wanted to see how you were.'

'That was kind. See you tomorrow.'

She smiled, but overcome by sudden weariness did not

get up to see him out. It was all she could do to clean her teeth and get into bed.

In the hall he ran into the elderly woman who was her landlady. He greeted her politely and made a swift exit. He wasn't tired, so decided to walk the few miles home.

It had turned into a fine night and the clouds had cleared to reveal stars and a crescent moon. As always, being with Fela stirred up feelings he'd thought forgotten. He admired her, not just for her beauty but for her courage and resourcefulness, and she aroused in him an immense tenderness. It wasn't the passion he'd once experienced and had no wish to feel again. In any case they would be moving on soon, most likely in different directions. More than ever, it was essential to keep his wits about him, undistracted by thoughts of some unimaginable future. He must concentrate his efforts on resolving the mess they were in.

———

The following morning Conrad knocked at Weiss's door, waited briefly and entered the room. Weiss was in the process of going through drawers and filing cabinets. He looked up in surprise.

'Did you knock?'

'I'm sorry. I thought maybe you hadn't heard me.'

'I've a plane to catch for Geneva,' Weiss replied shortly.

'When was this decided?'

'I had a phone call yesterday. HQ believe there's been a security leak. I'm going to discuss what steps we should take.'

'How long will you be away?'

'A couple of days. I'll keep you informed.'

'They're taking the theft of the vaccine very seriously then?'

'Of course. There'll be a thorough investigation.'

'We already know who's responsible. What else do they need to know?'

'I'm afraid it's not so simple. Others may be involved and need to be held accountable.'

Weiss was looking for a fall guy. That was obvious. He was off to Geneva to save his own skin.

'You're in charge till I get back,' said Weiss. 'My plane leaves in a couple of hours.'

Molly, his secretary, put her head round the door.

'Anything else you need, Dr Weiss?

'Yes, get those files to the shredder, would you. And these too.' He indicated a pile of papers on his desk. 'And order me a taxi.'

She nodded and disappeared.

'And what about Simon Eastlake's death? Do we just forget about that?'

'I received a report. The Garda have declared it an unfortunate accident. Reckless driving and falling asleep at the wheel. As far as I'm aware the case is closed.'

Conrad walked to the door. 'If there are plans to move the company from Ireland I hope you'll give us good notice. There are employees to consider and questions of compensation.'

'The days of the Unions are over, Dreyer! But don't worry, you'll be kept informed.'

He could hardly restrain his anger at Weiss's contemptuous attitude. If it was left to him, the company could pack up overnight without a thought to its workers, as long as he himself was okay. At least that was something Conrad was determined to prevent.

As he walked down the corridor, he did his best to calm his anger and think rationally. Weiss always played his cards close to his chest, but Conrad had a feeling that this time there was more to it. The company didn't usually go in for selling drugs through third parties. At one board meeting he'd attended, a senior executive had expressed the opinion that such dealings tarnished a company's reputation for very little financial reward. It was Weiss himself who had entered into discussions with the South Americans. What if he'd planned the deal for himself, and Jonas had beaten him to it? That might account for his fury.

He pulled out his mobile and dialled a number. 'Molly?' He was speaking softly. 'Can you hang onto those papers due for the shredder till I get a look at them? They may contain information I and others need.'

It was a risk requesting her to go behind her boss's back, but he knew she had a soft spot for him and resented the casual disdain with which Weiss treated her.

'I'll do my best,' she replied briskly, and the line went dead.

Back in his office he decided to go through R and D's financial records for the past two years with a fine toothcomb, focusing on any unusual or personal expenses.

Fela heard him come in and a moment later knocked at the communicating door and entered. The thought struck him that he might never see her again if the company was wound up.

'Is it true what people are saying?' she said. 'The whole place is buzzing with rumours they're moving us to Geneva.'

'HQ is furious about the sale of the vaccine. They believe there've been leaks. As boss, Weiss is responsible.'

'That doesn't answer my question.'

'I don't know the answer. He will no doubt find out.'

'Serve him right if they give him the third degree!'

'Unfortunately he's not committed any crime. Though in our line of work there's no such thing as crime. Only incompetence, and that's easily palmed off on others.'

'So we're to sit here and await our fate?'

'Looks like it.'

'Sometimes I wish I'd never taken this job!'

'Then we wouldn't have met. In my view it's one of the few good things to come out of this venture.'

He smiled but she didn't respond.

'I'm going through R and D expenses,' he said, resuming a more business-like tone. 'If you come across any invoices that aren't registered in the log, can you let me have them?'

She nodded and returned to her room.

Checking invoices against the records was the sort of painstaking work he hated. He opened his desk drawer and took out the bottle of Jameson's he kept there for emergencies; though it was only three thirty, he poured himself a shot.

By five he was still at it. He told Fela there was no need for her to stay any longer, since he intended to carry on for as long as it took. He returned to his task. Looking through the slim folder she'd handed him before leaving, he paused at an invoice that struck him as unusual. Two payments of 1500 euro had been made to Bond Pest Control Services. Anything to do with that sort of thing would normally be handled by Maintenance under Maloney, not R and D. He flicked through the rest of the pile and to his astonishment found another payment two days later to the same company for 5000 euro. His signature didn't appear on either invoice and he had no memory of authorising any such expenses. Perhaps Maloney could enlighten him. He decided to go down to his office.

He knocked at his door and getting no answer, pushed it open. Maloney was seated in front of a bank of TV security screens, though he wasn't watching any of them. Instead he appeared to be dozing, a can of beer open beside him.

'Maloney! Sorry to disturb you.'

He jumped at the sound of a voice and looked up. 'Dr Dreyer! Almost nodded off there. Been here since five this morning. How can I help you?'

'There's a small matter I need to clear up concerning R and D's expenses. Some items seem to have been accredited to us that I think should come under your section. Since they're quite large I need to check.'

Conrad handed him the invoices paid to Bond Pest Control.

After a pause Maloney shook his head.

'As you see they're for pest control. Some kind of infestation?'

'Sorry, Dr Dreyer, I know nothing of this.'

'Could you check your records to be sure?'

Maloney took down a ledger from the shelf and searched through it for the dates quoted on the invoices, but there was nothing.

'Dr Weiss did say to be extra vigilant,' he said as an afterthought.

'In general? Or about what?'

Maloney became more evasive. 'He was worried about certain things.'

'Dr Eastlake, for example?'

'Well, he asked me to keep an eye out.'

'The night Dr Eastlake went missing, did you see anything that concerned you?'

Maloney faced him like a rabbit caught in the head-lights. 'Like what?'

Conrad shrugged. 'Anything unusual?'

'I saw him going in and out of his lab. It was late, but often he worked late.'

'And you informed Dr Weiss?'

'He asked me to check, yes.'

'You saw him leave. Though it appears the CCTV camera cut out?'

'It does that sometimes.'

Mahoney turned away to replace the ledger on the shelf.

'Could someone have interfered with the CCTV footage?'

Maloney, increasingly uncomfortable, shook his head. 'I know nothing about that.'

'It's just that the camera failing around the time Dr

Eastlake left his lab and again on the entrance foyer seems like too much of a coincidence.'

Sensing Maloney's tension, he pressed on. 'Did you see if he was carrying a bag when he left his lab?'

Maloney hesitated for a second. 'I'd rather not say any more, Dr Dreyer. I don't want any trouble.'

'I understand. Just one more question. Is there any other way Dr Eastlake could have left the building?'

'Just the basement. There's a camera on the exit door but it's kept securely locked.'

'Thanks. Don't worry, I shan't mention our conversation to anyone else. Including Dr Weiss.'

As Conrad made his way back to his office, he went over what he'd learned. He was pretty sure Maloney had seen Simon leaving his lab, possibly with a bag. Now that footage was wiped. Conrad suspected he'd informed Weiss, as he'd been ordered to do, and it was Weiss who'd had the evidence destroyed, together with the footage of Simon leaving by the main entrance.

His thoughts returned to the invoices from Bond Pest Control. The size of the payments suggested some kind of special service. If neither he nor Maloney had authorised any such expenditure, it could only have been Weiss, who then attempted to bury it in R and D. What if he'd hired someone to follow Simon and take the hard drive? But if he had, why hadn't whoever it was returned it to him? He needed to find out more about Bond Pest Control.

———

W hen he got home Conrad googled the company. Their website offered to exterminate all infestations, including a follow up visit and two-year guarantee, starting at fifty euros up to three hundred for more serious cases. They gave an address just off the far end of O'Connell St. He decided to pay them a visit, citing an infestation of rodents.

The next morning being Saturday, he took the Dart into town and walked the length of O'Connell St. Eventually he came to a small turn off and followed the road past a Chinese takeaway, an off-licence with boarded up windows, and an electrical repair shop until he came to a row of rundown buildings. Bond Pest Control was in the end one. A faded blind covered the glass door, which had the company's logo on it. Conrad pushed it open and stepped in.

The place resembled a minicab office with the same indifference to décor or comfort. The walls were painted pistachio green and there was a high counter and a couple of hard chairs for people waiting. Seeing no one in attendance, Conrad pressed a bell marked 'Please ring for service'.

After a brief pause a woman appeared. In contrast to her unsavoury surroundings, she was attractive and smartly dressed, with well-cut blonde hair and careful makeup.

'Good morning, sir. How can I help you?' she said with a friendly smile.

'I believe you handle all sorts of infestations.'

'We do indeed. What kind have you in mind?'

'Rodents. I think it's rats.'

Her ample cleavage, half-hidden beneath a fitted jacket, was prominent enough to be a distraction.

'And what kind of location would that be?'

'My house. Close to a harbour, which I think encourages them.'

She nodded sympathetically. 'They love a drop of water.'

'I'd like them seen to as soon as possible.'

'Of course! Not the kind of little feet you want pattering round your old house now, is it, sir!'

She laughed merrily and he found himself smiling in response.

'Can I take your name and address?' She produced a pad and pencil from under the counter.

'Conrad Dreyer, 3 Harbour Cottages, Killiney.'

She wrote rapidly and with a swift movement tore the page from the pad. 'Take a seat, Mr Dreyer. I'll fetch one of our officers to have a chat with you.'

She disappeared into the back of the shop.

Conrad moved away from the counter but refrained from sitting down. He wondered if he should have given his real name and address, but it was too late now. He heard voices in the back, then a tall, thickset man of around forty dressed in jeans and leather jacket appeared.

'Mr Dreyer? I understand you've got rodent problems you'd like seeing to.'

'Yes. I've not yet seen a list of your charges.'

'That depends on the size of the problem. My receptionist says it's a house. Large or small?'

'Small, I'd say.'

197

'Unless it's a mansion, it'd be our regular charge of 200 euro. That includes a follow up visit to check the problem's been solved.'

'So when could you come?'

The man produced a ledger from under the counter and opened it up.

'How would next Friday suit you?'

'Fine.'

'Okay, Friday between two and five,' the man said as he wrote down Conrad's name, address and the date. 'I'm Jimmy, by the way. It'll be me or my colleague, Sean.'

He held out his hand to Conrad.

'See you Friday.'

He was about to go back inside when Conrad risked a further question.

'And if the problem wasn't just rats?'

The man paused and looked at him, weighing him up.

'What sort of additional problem?' he asked calmly.

Conrad held his gaze. 'Something bigger, needing a more skilled approach.'

There was another pause, then he said, 'Do you have a referral? We always like to check our clients' contacts.'

'Dr Weiss. Associated Swiss Pharmaceuticals.'

'Ah! Well, you'd have to speak to my colleague. He's the one for bigger problems. Leave me a number and I'll get him to call you.'

Conrad wrote down the number of his personal mobile and handed it to the man. 'I'll be waiting.'

The man's eyes followed him as he turned and left the shop.

· · ·

The air of O'Connell Street felt fresh after the atmosphere of Bond Pest Control. The place left him with a bad taste, as his rare brushes with the underworld usually did. The man had recognised Weiss's name, and the disparity between 200 euro for exterminating a few rats and the 8,000 Weiss had paid was proof enough that whatever contract he'd made with those people it didn't concern rats.

He didn't yet know how he'd respond to a call if one came, but in a sense it scarcely mattered. He wasn't likely to discover exactly what Weiss had requested, but it was a safe bet he'd hired someone to follow Simon into the mountains following Maloney's tip off, to take the hard drive Weiss believed he had with him. That the crash had proved fatal was probably a clumsy accident. But still the swiftness with which the police investigation had been abandoned bothered him.

Meanwhile he had to watch his own back. Having learned someone else had completed the sale he'd set up with the South Americans, Weiss would be looking for a scapegoat to save his skin. At a time when the company was already falling short of its financial targets, it'd had its most lucrative deal stolen from under its nose, proof if any were needed of the incompetence of its chief executive. Already implicated by seemingly having authorised the payments to Bond's, Conrad knew he was being set up. But he refused to be Weiss's fall guy.

There remained the question of Fela. Estelle had warned him not to get too involved, but he couldn't ignore what had happened between them. He couldn't walk away.

He pulled out his mobile and dialled her number. After a few rings she picked up.

'Hi. Are you busy?'

'Conrad! Not particularly. Just routine chores.'

'I thought I might pick you up in the Jeep. The weather's grand and we could drive along the coast or to the mountains.'

'To the lake?'

'If you like.'

'Give me an hour. I've a few things to finish first.'

'See you then.'

He rang off, his heart suddenly light.

————

A s the Jeep climbed into the hills, Conrad turned on the radio – Bob Dylan singing *Girl from the North Country*. They joined in at the tops of their voices. The sun came out from behind a passing cloud; she opened her window and felt the rush of wind on her face.

At the small car park on the crest of the hill, they packed the food they'd brought into rucksacks, locked the Jeep, and set off down the steep path to the lake. Fela looked down at the hut, searching for invaders, but there was no sign of activity.

When they reached the lake, Conrad unlocked and pushed open the door that stuck slightly on the earthen floor. The place was swept and tidy just as they'd left it, and it appeared no one else had been there since their previous visit. They unpacked the food, including two fine sea trout

Conrad had picked up from a local fisherman. He took a double sleeping bag from his backpack and unrolled it onto the makeshift bed then, though the day was still warm, set about making a fire. When the sun went down it would get chilly, and a fire would banish the lingering smell of damp.

Fela took off her clothes, under which she was already wearing her bikini, and ran out to the lake. She dived into the water, shouting out as the cold hit her, and struck off in a swift crawl. She swam a wide circle before returning to shore, shivering and triumphant. Conrad held out a towel and she wrapped herself up, stamping to restore the circulation in her feet.

'Wow! It's freezing!' She rubbed herself vigorously. 'Are you going in?'

'I suppose I'll have to.'

'You do indeed! I'll put the kettle on. Make us something hot to drink.'

She watched him pull off his jeans and sweatshirt and dive into the water, then went inside the hut.

When he came back, he was dressed and rubbing his wet hair with the towel. She handed him a mug of tea and they pulled up two chairs to sit in front of the fire. Her body still tingled from the swim and the tea was warm and comforting.

'How shall we cook the fish?' she asked.

'You're hungry already?'

'Starving!'

'We could put them on skewers and cook them over the fire.'

'Have we got skewers?'

'I can make some from green twigs. We can cook the fish over the embers.'

'Right. I'll peel the potatoes and do the salad.'

S he declared it the best meal she'd ever tasted. 'And the potatoes were boiled to perfection!'

'No need to humour me! I'm just the commie chef!'

He smiled. 'As long as we both know our stations.'

'For that, you do the washing up!'

Obediently he gathered up the plates and put on a kettle for hot water. She watched him as he went about his chores with practised efficiency.

When he'd finished, he brought out the whisky and offered her a dram. She shook her head and yawned. 'I think I'll go to bed.'

She undressed and slipped inside the sleeping bag. But away from the fire the bed felt cold and unwelcoming. She shivered. 'Come and warm me up!'

He took off his clothes and got in beside her.

'You're never cold,' she murmured. 'Even when your hair's still wet!'

He kissed her and ran his hands over her body. She moved closer into his embrace.

Afterwards they lay together, limbs entwined as though merged into a single being. The prospect of parting seemed to her an act of violence, impossible to contemplate.

'Is love too hard for you?'

Her voice, barely audible in the darkness, drew him back to consciousness. What could he answer? Love of comrade, child for parent or parent for child, though he'd never experienced the latter, these he recognised. But they were not what she wanted. Even if he proclaimed his deep fondness and the wholeheartedness of his desire, as rare in his view as that abused word 'love', that wouldn't satisfy her. He felt old and tired. There was so much he couldn't share, rough times and brutal actions in godforsaken corners of the earth, under orders but no less unforgivable, and the pain of betrayal and lost love. It would be like cramming too much cargo onto a fragile boat, only to capsize it.

'You have all of me that matters,' he said softly. 'The rest is of no account.' He stroked the damp hair from her face. 'Go to sleep.'

But the knowledge that he was the only one left she cared for weighed heavily. If he too were to disappear, she'd be alone. She raised her mouth to his, and as they kissed, the faint sound of an approaching helicopter penetrated the silence.

He sat up.

'What is it?'

The sound was coming closer, an ever increasing crescendo.

'I'll take a look.'

He pulled on his trousers and a sweater and opened the hut door.

A voice half-drowned by the roar of the hovering helicopter shouted over a loudhailer. 'Garda! Come forward slowly with your hands in the air!'

Conrad blinked in the beam of the searchlight as the chopper touched down and three armed officers got out and ran towards him, guns pointing, silhouetted against the light.

He put his hands behind his head but did not move. 'I'm not armed. There's no one here but me and Felicity O'Connor. You can search the hut. We've no weapons.'

His calmness seemed only to increase the tension of the young officers, who shifted from foot to foot. Their commander emerged, ducking his head against the wind of the rotors and gesturing to his men to lower their weapons.

'Conrad Dreyer, you're under arrest!'

'What for?'

'Fraud, industrial espionage and suspicion of homicide. You'll be formally charged at the station.'

Fela, dressed now, came to his side. She rested a hand on his shoulder.

'This is crazy!' she cried.

Conrad took her hand from his shoulder and held on to it. 'Best to co-operate. There's nothing we can do right now,' he said quietly. To the commander he said, 'Let me get our things. Your men can watch me if you want. There's no need to bring Miss O'Connor.'

'I want to come!' Fela said.

He turned to her. 'You'd better drive the Jeep back. I'll call you from the station.'

'Miss O'Connor is free to go,' the commander said.

'Where are you taking him?'

'Wexford Station,' the Sergeant replied. 'There's no need for you to come along.'

She stood watching as he was escorted to the helicopter. He climbed in, followed by the commander and three officers, and with a renewed burst of its engines the chopper corkscrewed upwards into the night sky.

A s soon as she reached the Jeep at the top of the hill, Fela called Estelle, the only person she could think of who might know what to do against such trumped-up charges. Estelle answered, instantly practical, and with a minimum of questions she went into action. She knew a good lawyer, who'd go down to Wexford first thing in the morning. In the unlikely case of Conrad being refused bail, the three of them would meet up to discuss further strategy.

'I agree Weiss is most likely behind this,' she said. 'But for the time being, it's best to keep any speculation to ourselves. The threat of losing their jobs may make some employees more willing to speak out.'

Fela turned the Jeep around and set off down the dark road for home.

———

C onrad stared at the greyish potatoes and two pink sausages congealing on a tin plate and pushed it aside. He took out his tobacco and rolled a cigarette. His anger had turned cold and his mind was sharp. He was due before the magistrate in the morning, after which he was pretty sure he'd be granted bail. He knew full well who was responsible for his arrest, and once free he'd go to work to get sufficient evidence to throw the guilt where it belonged.

At present all he had was the payment to Bonds, and he doubted he'd get anyone to testify to being hired to go after Simon and steal his hard drive. He felt increasingly sure Weiss had planned to profit personally from a deal with the South Americans. Why else be so keen to cover his tracks and look for someone else to incriminate?

The sergeant entered his cell and handed him his mobile phone. 'You're allowed one call,' he said.

He dialled Estelle, who answered at once.

'Conrad! Fela told me what's happened. A lawyer's on his way.'

Conscious of the sergeant's presence, he chose his words carefully. 'Thanks! I go before the Magistrate in the morning to ask for bail. If necessary can you go surety?'

'Of course. By the way, the lawyer's name is O'Gorman, Seamus O'Gorman.'

'Thanks again! I'll do the same for you one day!'

'Let's hope not!'

He handed the phone back to the sergeant.

'Can you tell me why I was brought all the way to Wexford?'

'It's the main station in the area.'

'I'd like to see the Chief Super.'

'He's not here, sir.'

'Tomorrow morning then. Before I go into court?'

'I doubt he'll be here then either. He's being transferred. We're awaiting the new chief.'

'Transferred?'

'Up the ladder. Assistant Commissioner. Next step it'll be The Castle itself!'

When the sergeant had left the cell, Conrad lay down

and pulled the thin blanket over him. He'd slept in worse places, and at least there were no cockroaches or bugs. Stretched out in the semi-darkness, he thought about the detective at the Wicklow Garda station, who'd so swiftly dismissed the possibility of suspicious circumstances and closed Simon's case. And here was the Chief Super of Wexford being singled out for promotion. It might be far-fetched, but he couldn't help wondering if there was some connection between the Garda and the company, or at least some influence being brought to bear. After all, it wasn't every day a helicopter and armed men were sent to pick up a relatively harmless criminal, almost certainly unarmed.

———

F ela slept badly and woke early. She got up and made a strong coffee. It was Monday and she should be leaving for work, though with Conrad absent no one would miss her. Until she heard from him, she couldn't think about anything else. She spent the morning cleaning the flat from top to bottom and finishing the ironing. At last a little after twelve her phone rang. She grabbed it.

'Conrad?'

'Yes.'

She almost wept with relief at the sound of his voice. 'What's the news?'

'I've been granted bail. An astronomical sum, but never mind.'

'Are you still at the court? I can drive down and get you.'

'I'll take the train. It's quicker. I'll be with you in a couple of hours. We'll talk then.'

'I'll be waiting.'

The line went dead. She stood where she was, the phone still clutched in her hand, overwhelmed by relief.

A couple of hours later, she was looking out of her window and saw him crossing the road with his long stride. She ran down the stairs and opened the door just as his finger touched the bell. She flung her arms round him then released him and stepped back.

'Come in! I've got food if you're hungry.'

Inside the flat she gestured him to sit down while she fetched the tray she'd prepared from the kitchen. He rubbed his hand over his face in a gesture of weariness as she set a plate of cold meat, bread, pickles and cheese down on the low table in front of him.

'Thanks! I didn't get much sleep last night. A police cell's not the best of billets.'

She put a bottle of beer down beside the tray. 'But you got bail!'

'Yes. Estelle stood surety.'

She felt a stab of jealousy, as she watched him lift the bottle to his lips and take a long swig.

'Thanks for this! Breakfast was porridge made with water, garda style, and a cup of weak tea. Still, it was hot.'

'At least you haven't got to spend another night there. So what now?'

'I'll go to the company. See what's going on.'

'Will they let you in?'

'I'll find out.'

She sat silently observing him, and thought how

quickly the intimacy of their lake visit had evaporated. Now, bent on hunting down his accusers, he'd withdrawn once more.

'Would you like coffee?'

'Later perhaps. What I'd really like is a short nap.'

'Of course. Take my bed. There's a clean towel in the shower.'

He got up, resting his hand in passing on her shoulder. 'I'm sorry you've been dragged into this. When it's over, I'll do my best to make it up to you.'

He went into the bedroom, closing the door behind him.

She was reading in the living room when he reappeared forty minutes later, showered and fresh. 'A new man!'

'I feel like one. I'd better get going.'

She went to her desk drawer and took out the keys to the Jeep.

'Best if you stay away from the company for the time being,' he said as she handed him the keys.

'Why? I mean you still have your job.'

'For today anyway. I need to find out when Weiss is back from Geneva.'

'And then?'

'I'll confront him. D'you want dinner later?'

'That'd be nice. I can cook. I've never cooked for you.'

'Let's go to your friend Maeve's. There'll be plenty more times for cooking.'

He bent down, kissed her on the cheek and was gone.

———

H e parked the Jeep in the car park and walked to the main entrance. He greeted the security guard, who didn't challenge him when he showed his pass, and the couple of people he passed on the corridor nodded their usual greeting. Perhaps word of his arrest hadn't yet reached them.

He took the lift to the top floor where Weiss had his office and paused outside to listen for voices. Hearing nothing, he knocked on the neighbouring door of Weiss's secretary. A voice said, 'Come in!'

Seated at her desk Molly O'Neill turned to greet him. Her face was puffy and it was clear she'd been crying.

'Dr Dreyer!' she exclaimed. 'I wasn't expecting you!'

'I presume you've heard what happened?'

She gestured him to a seat. 'No?'

'So can I ask what's upset you?'

'Dr Weiss. He called me first thing this morning. He never calls me at home or so early, so I knew it was urgent.'

She paused, struggling to master her emotions.

'From Geneva?'

She nodded. 'He was checking whether I'd shredded his documents, and when I said I was going to as soon as I got to the office, but they were safely locked in the cabinet, he became absolutely furious, shouting and using language I've never heard before. He kept saying if there were consequences, he'd make sure I'd regret it. I didn't know what he was talking about.'

'That must have been very upsetting.'

'I've always worked hard and done my best for him.'

She mopped her eyes with a handkerchief. 'I'm sorry. I'm not usually like this.'

'No, no! It's my fault for asking you to hang on to them.'

She shook her head. 'I've worked here five years, four for Dr Weiss. No one's ever spoken to me like that!'

'Did he say anything about what had upset him – apart from the shredding?'

'He said he'd been betrayed by his colleagues, especially you, and if anyone was responsible for the company's losses, it was you and you'd pay for it. He even suggested I'd been feeding you privileged information, and when I told him I'd never done anything of the kind, he shouted back, "So who else had access to my files? Tell me that!"'

Conrad pulled a clean cotton handkerchief from his pocket and handed it to her to replace the soggy shred of paper she was clutching. He waited for her to grow calmer then said, 'You know the best way to respond to abuse?'

She looked at him, bleary eyed.

'Look for what lies behind it! It's me Weiss is really angry with. With you he's just a bully letting off steam. I need to open those files and see what's in them.'

'You think that's safe?'

'I'll make sure of it. And whatever happens, I'll take the blame.'

'The truth needs to come out!'

'It does indeed!'

She searched in her desk drawer and produced a bunch of keys, which she handed to him.

'Go home, have a drink and a good dinner, Molly, and

forget all about Weiss. From now on he's my responsibility.'

She gave him a watery smile.

'You're a good man, Dr Dreyer. You don't deserve this.'

He smiled, touched by her faith. At the door to Weiss's
office, he paused.

'Does he have CCTV in there?'

She shook her head. 'He had the camera removed a few
months ago. Said there was no need for it.'

'Perhaps he wants to make sure no one keeps an eye on
him! I'll return the keys to your drawer when I leave.'

'Thanks, Dr Dreyer. And good luck!'

He smiled at her. 'You're great at your job, Molly, and
don't ever forget it!'

She gathered up her coat and bag and left her room
with a watery smile and a wave of her hand.

He entered Weiss's office, keeping the door to the
corridor locked. To the left of the desk was a strong cabinet. He found the relevant key, unlocked it, pulled out the
files and laid them on the desk.

His phone went. He glanced at the name of the caller,
and saw it was Fela.

'I just met Molly in the car park. Are you in Weiss's
office?'

'I can't talk right now.'

'You might as well because I'm coming up.'

Fela was the last person he needed right now, but he
knew she wasn't about to be put off.

'Okay. But if anyone sees you, don't come here but go
straight to your own room.'

'I'll be careful.'

A few minutes later there was a gentle knock at the door. He unlocked it and Fela entered. He locked it again behind her and pocketed the key. She gazed at the files piled up on the desk.

'Looks like you need all the help you can get! What exactly are we looking for?'

He hesitated for a moment then said, 'Any document, letter, agreement or financial transaction that has to do with the vaccine or Guatemala.'

They set to work putting the files into separate piles, taking one each and starting with the most recent. At first neither found anything of interest, and eventually Conrad suggested taking a short break. There was a coffee machine and some biscuits in Molly's office. Ten minutes later they returned to Weiss's office and resumed their task.

At length Conrad turned up a letter from an official in the Guatemalan government referring to the potential sale of the vaccine, though nothing incriminating.

'We need to collect any personal correspondence between Dr Weiss and anyone from Guatemala,' said Conrad.

'There's a diary on Molly's desk. Maybe that shows something.'

She fetched it and ran through the first few pages, then paused at an entry in March, barely three weeks ago.

'Look! There's something here, written in pencil that someone's tried to rub out.'

She handed him the diary.

He held the page under the lamp and peered at it closely. 'Perez, golf club 12.30.'

He moved on to the following page. 'Aha!'

'What?'

'"Bond Pest Control to R and D." This must be a note to Molly to send the invoice to us for payment.'

She looked confused. 'Pest as in rats and cockroaches? What's that to do with us?'

'I found a payment to them for 8000 euros in our accounts.'

'8000! That's news to me.'

'You keep a cheque book in your desk for emergencies, don't you?'

She nodded.

'When you get back, see if any of the stubs have been left blank.'

'D'you believe he'd do that?'

'I'd believe anything of him.'

In the next file she picked up, Fela came across another letter from someone in the Guatemalan embassy and handed it to Conrad. It was written in casually friendly terms, and mentioned a forthcoming assignation but no time or place. He put the letter on one side, together with several other documents he'd selected, and looked at his watch. It was almost six. The building would be emptying, but Maloney might come up to investigate if he saw a light. He drew the blinds and switched on the desk lamp, which gave a more localised light.

'I'm sure he won't, but if Weiss did come back just go to Molly's room and keep out of sight. I'll deal with him.'

She nodded. She was enjoying their adventure.

A few minutes later she held up another letter. 'This

might interest you. It's from the man mentioned in the diary, Perez.'

She handed the letter to Conrad.

Miguel Perez thanked Dr Weiss for his invitation to the annual Culture Night dinner at the Freemasons' Hall in Dublin, to which he was looking forward.

'"It is especially gratifying to be meeting in such a fine and time-honoured place. I'm sure we will be able to work out an agreement to both our advantages,"' Conrad read out loud. 'So Weiss is a Freemason!'

'Is that relevant?'

'It might be. They're an international organisation, well known for their networking skills. Connections that give special privileges to their members.'

Suddenly there was the sound of footsteps approaching along the corridor. It was most likely Maloney but they both froze. Finger on lips, Conrad gestured to Fela to return to Molly's office and switched off the lamp. She did so, quietly closing the communicating door behind her. He waited, as the footsteps stopped and there was the sound of a key being inserted in the door. It was too late to escape.

The door opened and Weiss entered. He didn't see Conrad until he switched on the light then started back in shock. 'Dreyer! What the hell are you doing here?'

'Dr Weiss.'

'What are you doing in my office? I'm sending for security.'

He strode over to the desk and reached for the phone, but Conrad intercepted him, grabbing his wrist. Weiss winced at the strength of his grip. After a moment Conrad let go and Weiss took a step back.

'First you're going to talk to me.'

Weiss glared at him but said nothing. He was neither a strong nor courageous man.

'Was it your idea to send armed guards and a helicopter to arrest me?'

'Trespassing on company property and harassing me contravenes the conditions of your bail, I believe. If you leave now, I won't inform on you.'

Conrad gave a snort of contempt. 'You think you can make me take the rap for your failed attempts at fraud? So you can return to Geneva freed from all responsibility?'

Weiss held his gaze. 'You will go to jail for the crimes you've committed, Dreyer.'

There'd been times when Conrad had allowed rage to get the better of him, but now he was in full control. 'You know that whatever crimes have been committed, they're not by me,' he said icily.

'Then who is the culprit?'

For a moment Conrad said nothing.

Taking his silence for weakening, Weiss grew more confident. 'You stole company property and sold it off, together with your accomplice, Jonas Finzi, for your own illicit gain. I'm open to evidence to the contrary, if you have any.'

Convinced as Conrad was of Weiss's guilt, he had only circumstantial evidence, not enough to stand up in court against some fancy lawyer. He thought of the poker games he'd played with his fellow soldiers to while away many a restless night waiting for action. He'd enjoyed pretending he had a better hand than he did, stretching out the tension in a game of nerves. He reached for the letters from the Guatemalan embassy man and ran his eye over the most recent one.

'How long have you been a member of the Freemasons?'

Weiss gave a snort of contempt. 'Oh, please! Not that old chestnut! Freemasons part of a secret, self-serving brotherhood!'

'Brotherhoods exist to do each other favours.'

'Our reputation for charitable works is also well known.'

'If you mean looking after your own. You used your connections to make a deal with a brother from Guatemala, a government official. Were you planning to take all the profits, or just cream off a nice little sum for yourselves without the company realising?'

'The deal was open and above board, as you well know.'

'Except with you in charge it had run into trouble. After you'd taken your cut, the rewards would be considerably less. And so HQ were considering cutting their losses and pulling out of Ireland. And then Dr Eastlake threatened to destroy his research.'

Weiss's face had grown flushed but he said nothing.

'Is the ex-Chief Super of Wexford Garda Station also part of your "brotherhood"?'

For the first time, Weiss appeared to have difficulty controlling himself. 'What exactly are you implying?'

'I hear he's been made an Assistant Commissioner. A top job for the price of ordering evidence to be overlooked and assisting a fellow "brother" to detain a wanted criminal.'

Weiss could no longer contain his anger. 'You'd better be careful what you say. I have powerful friends in this city. You're only digging a deeper hole for yourself.'

'I don't doubt it. But Ireland isn't a banana republic. The law is still independent, and considers the evidence put before it. You can threaten me, but when the evidence I have is presented in court you, will have to answer for it.'

'What evidence?' Weiss's voice rose almost to a scream. He made a grab for the letters, but Conrad was taller and more agile, and shifted them out of his reach.

'I have written testimony, not only of the deal you made over the vaccine, but of your hiring men to follow Dr Eastlake to the mountains, resulting in his death.'

He took his phone from his pocket, and showed Weiss the photo he'd taken of the damage to the rear of Simon's car. Weiss made no comment.

'Speaks for itself, I think. Any of those involved, including your pal the Chief Super, can be forced to testify in court, and believe me, it won't look good for you.'

Weiss remained silent. He wasn't yet beaten but fear for his own skin was making him question any reckless desire for a fight. If Conrad had what he claimed it might be necessary to come to an agreement.

'So what exactly are the terms of your blackmail?' he said coldly.

'You drop all charges against me.'

'And blame who for the crimes you committed?'

'Jonas Finzi, if you like, for stealing the research and

selling the vaccine. You've already made sure Simon East-lake's death was dismissed as an accident. So case closed. You can return to your bosses in Geneva, reputation intact. But remember, if you send me to prison, one day I'll be out, and I swear to God I'll find you.'

Weiss held his gaze for a moment. Knowing Conrad's background, what he said was no idle threat, and since he'd offered him a way out, he saw little point in risking personal harm.

'You always were a thug!' he spat out and turned to the door.

'Lock up before you go. And I suggest you leave via the car park. You don't want to be caught trespassing.'

Conrad listened to his footsteps receding down the corridor.

The communicating door opened and a whispered voice said, 'Has he gone?' Fela stood in the doorway.

He'd forgotten she was there, and thanked heaven Weiss hadn't got wind of her presence.

'God, he's a liar! You've got me as witness. I'm sure if we go on searching, we can come up with more evidence.'

He smiled, touched by her indignation. 'Let's see first if he withdraws the charges.'

'He's guilty as hell, though I wouldn't trust him as far as I could throw him! And that would be a lot farther than Geneva!'

'He's also a coward. All he wants is to save his own skin. Let's get out of here. You leave first. I'll follow and meet you at Maeve's.'

'He won't get away with this. Whatever happens, we'll see that he doesn't!'

She kissed him briefly on the lips then returned to Molly's office, picked up her coat and bag and closed the door behind her.

Conrad extinguished the lamps in Weiss's office and stood waiting in the darkness for the sound of her footsteps to fade before locking up. He wasn't proud of what he'd done. Telling Weiss to blame Jonas, even though he'd finally been the one to sell off the vaccine, and letting him get away with Simon's death went badly against his conscience. But the case against him was too flimsy, and given greater provocation Weiss would be forced to defend himself with whatever it took. He couldn't pretend, as Jonas had tried, that the end justified the means. It was another fudge, a compromise with truth and justice in the name of expediency, that left a bad taste whichever way he looked at it. Scientific research could not be chained by rules, but its uses should at least be debated. That was what Simon demanded, with catastrophic consequences. He had neither Simon's reckless courage nor youthful idealism, and to avoid being made Weiss's scapegoat, he'd sacrificed what remained of his conscience. It was time to bow out.

There was only one remaining problem, and that was Fela. It had suited him to encourage her affections, and he could not abandon her now. She was committed to finding justice for Simon, a cause they'd undertaken together. She would never let go. No matter how great the risk of going up against the limitless resources of ASP, like David against Goliath, she believed fearlessness and tenacity would prove a match for might. And whilst he feared for her, he wished with all his heart she might be right.

He gathered up the files he'd earmarked from Weiss's desk and shoved them into his backpack, replaced the cabinet keys in Molly's desk drawer and locked both office doors behind him. On his way out, he stopped to wish Maloney goodnight. Absorbed in a rugby match, Maloney kept his eyes glued to the screen, waving a hand in response. Conrad hung Weiss's keys on the appropriate hook and, feeling suddenly light-hearted, left the building for what might well be the last time.

———

Maeve's was already crowded when he arrived. Fela had found a corner table and was reading a book. She looked up as Conrad approached and greeted him with a welcoming smile.

'No one stopped you then?'

'Maloney was lost in the rugby. I met no one else.'

'We make a good team, don't we!'

He smiled his agreement.

'That bastard Weiss! We'll see he gets what he deserves!'

'Alas, I wouldn't bet on it.' He took the seat opposite her. Maeve came over and set a large glass of red in front of him.

'You look as if you need that!' she said. 'Dish of the day's jugged hare. Will that do you both?'

'Perfect!'

Fela agreed, and Maeve disappeared into the kitchen.

'He won't if we do nothing,' Fela said. 'I believe with what we have and what more we may unearth, it'll be possible to convict him. You'll see, when his crimes are exposed, his company masters will be only too keen to disassociate themselves.'

'It's a long shot.'

'Maybe, but if we can find a good lawyer, someone who relishes this kind of fight, that's a start. And once the case gets known, others may be willing to come forward as witnesses.'

'And how do we pay a lawyer?'

'In a case of this significance, there are some who are prepared to take deferred payment. Estelle will know.'

'For the crime of murder, or selling untested vaccines through third parties?'

'Both. Which is why ASP won't defend him, for the sake of their own reputation!' Her optimism was infectious. 'So do we go for it?'

She stretched out her hand, and after a brief hesitation he pressed his palm to hers. 'What've we got to lose!'

Maeve appeared with their food. 'You're in for a treat tonight!' she said as she set it down before them.

'Yes! Tell him!' Fela said excitedly.

'The Cleary brothers are playing, with their young nephew, Eamon, on percussion. It promises to be a grand night!'

'The Clearys from Castlebar?'

'That's the ones!'

'A treat indeed!'

'I'm glad you appreciate it,' Maeve said and went on her way.

Fela raised her glass to his. 'Tonight I want to eat, drink and be merry!'

'Here's to a brighter future!'

As they ate, Conrad told her about his night in the cells, and how impressed he was with the magistrate's quick grasp of events and authoritative way of dealing with the Garda. Whatever corruption was involved, he wasn't part of it.

They were onto their second bottle of wine when the musicians arrived, keyboard player, bass guitar, violin, and a lad looking no more than sixteen on percussion. They set up on a small stage at the back of the room, while everyone stood up and Maeve and the barman moved tables around to make space. More people began arriving, till there was standing room only.

'Conrad Dreyer! I didn't expect to see you here,' a cheery voice greeted him.

Conrad turned and for a moment scarcely recognised Charlie. She was dressed smartly in striped shirt and black jeans, and her hair, hitherto hidden under a cap, hung down her back in a thick plait the colour of ripe corn.

'Are you here for the music?'

She nodded. 'They're one of my favourite bands!'

She turned to Fela. 'Are you going to introduce me?'

'Fela O'Connor, daughter of the great Sean O'Connor.'

'Wow! Another of my heroes!' She held out her hand. 'I'm truly sorry for your loss.'

Fela took her hand. 'And how do you two know each other?'

'Conrad had better explain. Maybe we can catch up later?'

'Sure.' She watched Charlie make her way back to a

table, where another young woman and two young men were seated.

'She seems nice!'

'Yes.'

'So tell me about her.'

'She belongs to an organisation that looks into the dodgy dealings of pharma companies.'

'An eco warrior?'

'Call them that, if you want. They seem to be honest people.'

'I don't doubt it. So how did you meet her?'

'I was trying to find out who was selling the vaccine. Estelle introduced me.'

'And they were able to tell you?'

'I was too late. The guy in question was already leaving the country.'

Fela was silent for a moment. 'I'd like to know more about such an organisation.'

'Then Charlie's the one to speak to.'

'You've got her number?'

He nodded.

The musicians finished tuning up. The guitarist counted them in, and they set off at a brisk pace to the acclaim of the crowd. They played ballads and rebel songs and wild reels that got everyone up and dancing. At one point Fela pulled Conrad onto the floor, and he leapt and roared with the best of them.

'Remind you of anyone?' Fela shouted, gesturing at the fiddle player.

'Almost as good as your da!' he yelled back.

Her eyes were bright, but not with tears.

As they danced, she suddenly found herself side by side with Charlie and tapped her on the shoulder.

'Mind if I give you a call sometime?' she shouted in her ear. 'I'd like to know more about what you do.'

Charlie grinned. 'Better watch out. We might end up converting you!'

I t was after one when the musicians announced their final number, *Raglan Road*, a haunting favourite with the crowd, and the mood quietened. When it was done, the people thanked Maeve and the musicians, declaring over and over it had been a night to remember.

Outside, Fela and Conrad walked arm in arm down the dark street through the gradually thinning crowd.

'I love this country!' Fela said. 'One day I guess I'll settle here.'

'But first?'

She didn't reply at once, and they walked on in silence.

'Africa, maybe,' she said at length. 'Once Weiss has got his deserts... Perhaps I'll speak to Charlie.' She paused, lost in her own thoughts.

'My Grandmother's garden was full of flowers. Especially the orange, yellow and dark red Canna Lilies and Crane Flowers. She loved them best because of the humming-bird moths that came to suck their sweetness. In the afternoons, I'd lie with my mother in a hammock under the jacaranda tree, watching white clouds like ships in full sail drift across the infinite blue sky. I thought I was in paradise!'

Prompted by her words, Conrad's thoughts drifted to

Somalia, the last posting of his soldiering life – its harsh landscape, wild canyons and barren mountains behind which the sun set so magnificently. He heard again the cries of the camel herders with their great loads of grasses, and the distant snatches of a woman's song as she walked the endless miles from nowhere to nowhere with her white goat, her face half-covered by a bright blue shawl. But such memories aroused no nostalgia. They belonged to the past, unlike Fela's - relics to which there was no possibility of return.

He glanced at her rapt young face, lost in dreams. He would never forget the crossing of their paths, but soon it would be time to go their separate ways.

She stopped suddenly and pointed upwards. 'Look!' she exclaimed, gripping his arm.

Above them the clouds had parted, revealing the Milky Way in all its vastness, an infinity of stars that filled the night sky. They stood together in shared wonder, gazing upwards at the miracle that was the universe.

THE END

ABOUT THE AUTHOR

Jane Corbett studied History and English at Newham College, Cambridge, and is the author of a literary novel *Looking for Home*, a YA novel *Out of Step*, a volume of modern fairy tales entitled *Beasts and Lovers*, and several award winning screenplays. In the 70s and 80s she ran filmmaking workshops and taught at the progressive Kingsway College. More recently she has taught storytelling and documentary filmmaking at the National Film and Television School. She lives in London with her extended family.

www.janecorbett-writer.com

Lightning Source UK Ltd.
Milton Keynes UK
UKHW011432260820
368861UK00003B/1015